COVER-UP

ORLANDO KIMBER

The Arthur & Moose
Publishing Company

ABOUT THE AUTHOR

Orlando grew up in London, played guitar, and worked as a music producer and composer for tv and film.

He moved into international broadcasting, and led campaigns for the Digital Revolution of the BBC, and the launch of the internet in Europe. Subsequently, he lived and worked in the Middle East.

A new chapter started in 2012, when his wife fell seriously ill. Together, they moved to Cornwall, where she has family roots. Orlando began writing and campaigning for both ethical governance, and protection of the natural environment.

Orlando produces popular non-fiction and fiction.

Copyright © 2023 by Orlando Kimber

The right of Orlando Kimber to be identified as the author of this work has been asserted by him in accordance with the Copyright, Designs and Patents Act 1988.

All rights reserved.

No part of this publication may be reproduced in any form or by any electronic or mechanical means, including information storage and retrieval systems, without prior written permission from the author.

This is a work of fiction. Names, characters, businesses and events are the products of the author's imagination. With respect to such creations, any similarity to a name, character, business or event, is entirely coincidental and unintentional.

ISBN of the print edition is 978-1-915019-02-8

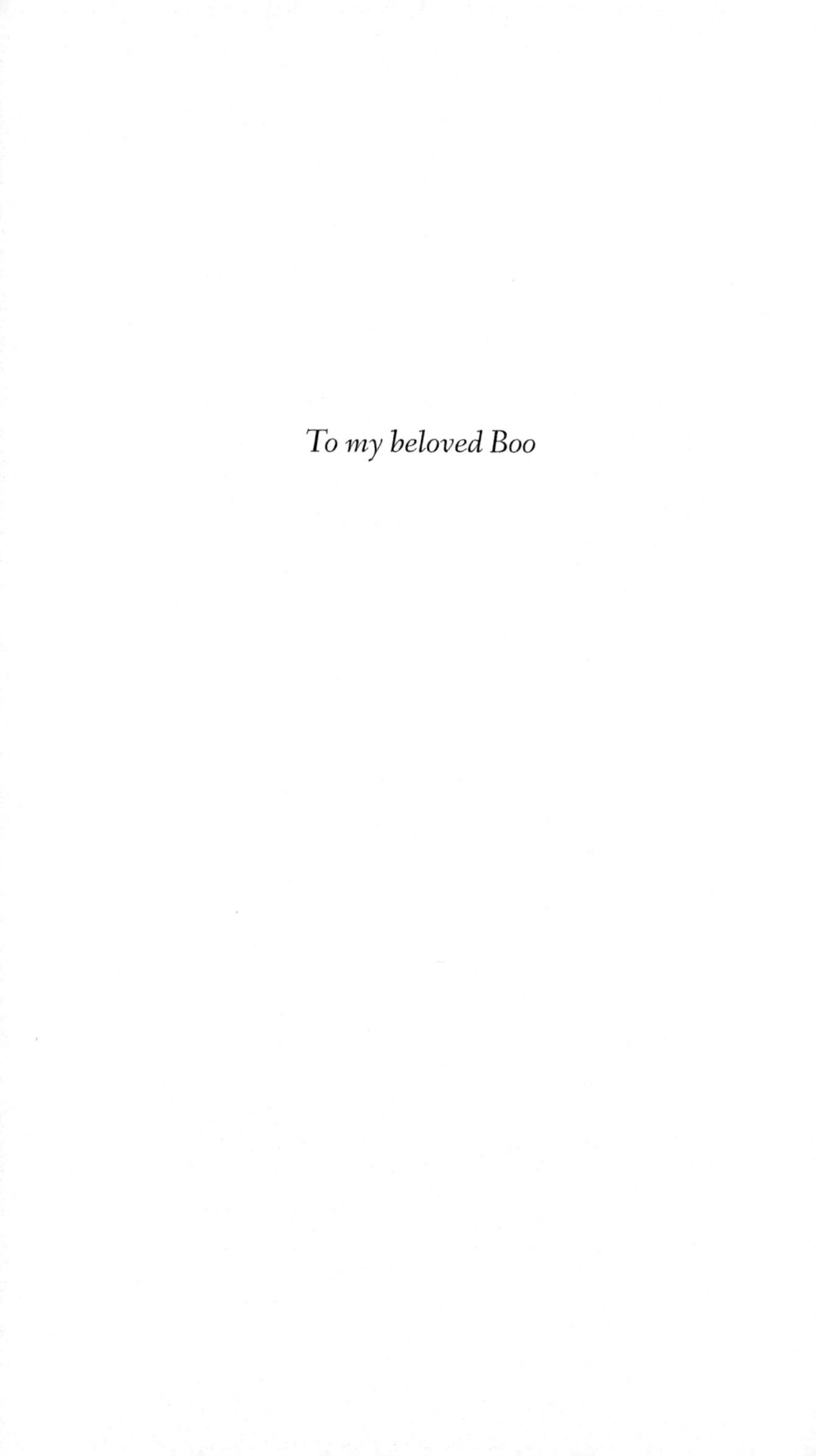

To my beloved Boo

CONTENTS

1

PINNED

Saul can't open his left eye. It's glued shut. The heat is stifling and it's hard to breathe. Thirst. The air rasps in his throat and the left side of his head rings with pain. Gradually, it dawns on him ... an accident on his bike.

He is pinned to the ground. He feels the dry grit beneath his hands. The weight of the motorbike is enormous; the vast heap of machinery flattening his torso on the baked, unyielding earth. Absurdly, Saul visualizes the bike's weight, printed in the driver's manual. Six hundred and four pounds: four times his body mass in hot metal.

His skull aches inside and out; every fractional head movement is a small explosion of pain. His whole body feels like one enormous bruise. His throat pulses with hurt. *How could the strap have broken on my helmet?* Agonizingly, he turns to the right and glimpses it, five metres away. *Where are my gloves?*

Saul strains to lift the machinery clear of his body. By bracing himself, he shifts the bike from his right leg. The machine pivots to his left and out of control, compressing his chest with even greater ferocity. His left shoulder screams at him. As he gasps, he involuntarily throws his head back to the dirt. Mistake. He fights back the urge to vomit.

Saul tries to go limp and use his mind; he squints at the August sun, as it beats down from high above. He opens his mouth to shout for help, but the only noise he hears is a faint groan. The pain of the effort sends him into momentary shock. He hopes someone will find him soon, and then realizes that someone has ...

2

SPIKED

The atrium is of steel and marble, with extravagantly comfortable, low armchairs. It states – no, bellows – *money*. National broadsheets are not meant to be distracted by glamour: they are temples of truth-telling. They're founded on solid evidence tempered by the time-honoured values of justice, fairness and equity. Here, journalists once gathered bundles of salient facts, scrutinized them for freshness, relevance and accuracy, and then subjected their judgement to the fierce heat of self-criticism. Such preparations were made in the knowledge that great and good decision-makers need solid nourishment.

Not so *The Inquirer* in the twenty-first century, where big money has oozed into so many crevices and across so many surfaces. A large investment has provided lubrication for online adventures and, thus, a significant return of capital is naturally demanded.

Nowadays, the many pages are filled with a salad of half-digested hearsay. Facts are tossed, with a sprinkling of opinions and crumbs of historic data, to ensure the smack of credibility. If the astringent vinegar of truth is too strong, it's sweetened with the oil of commercial expediency. The result is pap. Fashionable policy-makers, and even government ministers, can then regurgitate this on talk shows, designed for the maximum number of politically correct urban consumers.

However, at *The Inquirer* newspaper, there is at least one exception.

He seldom rides the gleaming stainless-steel lift to the sixth floor, where the directors reside, in cloistered comfort, at the end of a softly carpeted corridor.

Below, on the second floor, the editor has summoned him to a meeting in her polished, frosted-glass, rose-scented cubicle. From here, she overlooks a newsroom on one side, and the toiling London traffic on the other. Fortunately, the triple-glazed windows keep her sealed from the inconvenient din of the real world.

'It's good work. I mean it. Really first class. But we can't run it ... not yet.'

Saul's jaw opens in disbelief, the question mark obvious.

Natalie Curzon-Watson stares directly at her charge. As a seasoned editor of a national broadsheet, she's used to telling journalists things they don't want to hear. It's at times like this that she feels grateful for her habit of dressing immaculately; as though the slightest error in her business attire would give permission for criticism of her judgement. 'Yes, you've done your research. Yes, I gave you freedom to write the story as you saw fit and yes, it's powerful stuff. But we're not ready.' She fights the urge to drop her eyes to the screen; her junior investigative reporter shows no sign of yielding. Much as she wants the story to break, her bosses have closed their boardroom door on it. They've made it clear that no increase in readership will compensate for the possible cost of a legal challenge. Apparently, *The Inquirer*'s debt repayments from the corporate restructuring have left them temporarily short. They are forcing her to back down.

'With the greatest respect, Natalie, what the fuck?'

She raises a single eyebrow. Saul is one of the few journalists in her charge that she considers truly civilized. *Perhaps it's just that damn accent; perhaps it's his clean-cut charm*, she thinks. Natalie allows the silence to continue, so Saul can reflect on what he's just said. Then, 'I'm the only one who gets to swear in here.' Despite seventeen years as an

American in Britain, she still hasn't mastered their sense of irony.

'No, really, what the hell are you talking about? This took me the best part of six months. You commissioned it, I've kept you posted, we've spent money on this and you're spiking it? Now?'

'Not spiking it, Saul, we need more information.' Her strong jaw presses forward.

The lean, young man throws himself back in the fake-leather seat, gripping the chrome arms. His knuckles whiten, in the effort of dissipating his fury.

'What do you expect me to do? What do you need from me?'

'It's a case of timing. New data's come in, which puts your story in a totally different light.'

'So tell me about it.'

'I can't.'

'Excuse me? We're desperate for a big story like this. There have been mine attacks on naval assets worldwide. There are conspiracy theories all over the internet, and yet we've got the scoop on who and why ... uncovered at personal risk. You're telling me you're suppressing it for something 'more important'? I've shown this is Russian infiltration into the UK, at the highest level. If it's relevant to the story, I need to know, Natalie. Now.'

'We're checking it out.'

'You can't be serious?'

'Do I need to remind you this is a matter of

national importance? Since when did you think we were above the law, boy wonder?'

'That's the point, and you know it. Our corridors of power are threaded with corruption, and this one goes all the way to the top. We can prove it all goes back to Bovar and his friends.'

'And another thing: we have to cover off the legals.'

'You know we've covered our arses to the max. You know this is bullshit.'

'Careful, Saul. If you want to crusade, you do so on your own dollar.'

It's too late. A frozen wasteland of distrust yawns between them.

Natalie waits a beat. 'OK, this isn't happening. Take a few days off. Paid leave, we'll call it. Come back when you're ready.' She purses her lips, staunching the ready flow of words that rise and lap within. She groans inwardly at her own repression of feelings. *So damn British*, she thinks, *they've got to me*.

Saul shoves the chair back, turns and strides out of the office.

3

LOGE

Two pigeons perch precariously on the closest of the two parallel wires that run the length of Podolskaya Ulitsa. The elegance of the surrounding buildings – none more than a few storeys – gives a stately dignity to the area. Years of neglect have jaded their former glory. It's a broad way, and even now, in the early evening, there's little to disturb the urban air; just the occasional tram.

Warm, golden sunlight favours the room. Loge is proud to live in the same street in which Dmitri Dmitriyevich Shostakovich had been born. The great man's father had – like Loge – studied physics and mathematics at St Petersburg University. Like him, Loge had gone on to be an engineer. Once upon a time, Loge too had found the full satisfaction of his high ideals, fine intellect and will for order in the joy of science and technology. That now seems long ago.

Thirsting strings and strident timpani bring Shostakovich's fifth symphony to a close, and he removes his headphones. He takes the record from the turntable, and places it reverently back in its inner and outer sleeves. Tears still course down his grey-pink cheeks as he remembers his beloved grandparents, and the loss of so much he still holds dear. Another era. He sits absolutely still on the firm desk chair, his veined, seventy-year-old hands resting heavily on wooden arms, smoothed by decades of use. To Loge, the music is an agonizingly prolonged plea to remember our humanity – our need for freedom, affection, family and nature – in the onslaught of 'progress'. Throughout his career, he has fought silently for this. Commercial forces routinely betray the old ideals of Communism of course, despite their protestations to the contrary.

In the dimming light, he allows his sight to linger on the silver and wooden-framed images of his son and daughter. Victor, in military uniform, passing out from the military academy. Elena in an open-necked blouse, writing with pen and paper, at a picnic table in the woods, sun streaming through the leaves around her.

He longs for a cigarette. Despite decades of sitting in smoke-filled conference rooms with other dark-suited men, he never succumbed. *No, I won't smoke, but I will play chess.* He leans forward and extends the knotted middle finger of his left hand to pull a scrap of yellow paper towards him. He has written 'o-o', a reminder of his likely next move, a kingside castle. The game is long past the opening.

He hears his wife moving about in the kitchen downstairs, preparing a late supper for them both, after her trip to the hospital. Moving to the screen, he sees Johns is online and sends a chat message in English:

Play?

Certainly.

Online chess has been one of the very few joys in Loge's life in recent years. To find worthy opponents such as Johns, in far-flung corners of the earth, was a constant delight. Indeed, they are so closely matched that their relationship has taken on a life of its own. More valuable in some ways than those Loge endures in his everyday work and home lives. It is ironic that these particular games have taken on such importance.

The phone rings. He answers it, softly cursing the timing.

'Papa, Elena here.'

'Darling, how good to hear you. One moment.' Loge sends a message to Johns:

Five minutes? Calls with his family never last long.

Good, comes the reply.

'I'm back, Elena. How are you?'

'Excellent, Papa, excellent. Will you and Mother

come to Moscow at the end of the month for the presentation? I need to let the organizers know.'

'I'm sorry, to what are you referring?'

'Mother hasn't told you? The award? I'm to receive the Anna Politkovskaya Award.'

'No, she hasn't mentioned it. Tell me.'

'It's only an international award to honour women human rights defenders from around the world.'

'They've chosen you?' He bites his lip as he realizes how dismissive this sounds.

'I understand why you may be surprised, given your line of work.'

'Now, Elena, please don't be like that.'

'It's clearly of no interest to my parents that their daughter is recognized publicly for her work as a campaigner.'

'Perhaps your mother is anxious about your safety?'

'So she didn't bother to tell you about the presentation?'

'I've been very busy.'

'Ha, the story of my life. Just let me know, OK? Goodbye, Papa.'

'Elena—' but it's too late.

He puts the phone down, looks once more at the image of his daughter in sunlight, and then returns to the glow of his screen. Dusk has come now, and left his study in a gloom of dark wood.

Back.

Johns has moved. A typically subtle and intelligent play, aimed at trapping Loge's queen.

I see the truth of your position, writes Loge.

No reply. He smiles wryly; the ebb and flow of the two men's comments have become almost as significant to him as the game itself. He throws the yellow note into the bin, and counter-attacks. For some reason, Moravec's paradox comes to mind, 'Machines are good where humans are weak.' He detests the ambiguity in this, positing ethical conduct in reference to the simple strength of an automaton. As an engineer, Loge admires the power, precision and endurance of a mechanism, and his one indulgence in life has been to buy a few modest pieces of Futurist art. However, as a man who grew up in the Soviet era, he had concluded long ago that there were limits to the usefulness of machines. The direct playing of chess moves by computer is one such breach of propriety. The game is a competition between human minds; that a computer may be stronger is irrelevant to this purpose.

The door opens. His wife, Valerie. She is wearing a bright blue-and-white floral apron. It distracts from her red forehead, exposed by a plastic band that draws back her badly-dyed hair. It suggests a brash forcefulness, totally at odds with the domestic charm of her attire.

'Supper is ready.'

'Thank you, darling. I'm coming.'

'I want a new dress. You promised me one.'

Her blunt approach surprises Loge. The Russian word *bestaknyy* ... brusque, seems to capture it perfectly.

'Of course, darling. Let's discuss it over dinner.'

'There is nothing to discuss.'

'I'll be with you in just a minute.'

The door closes as abruptly as it opened. Loge breathes deeply, trying to dispel the resentment he feels at the invasion of his inner sanctum, and the interruption to his thoughts.

Duty calls.

Got it.

4

JOHNS

Dmitri Johns is amused by his opponent's move. Loge appears to believe in his feint towards the queen, and has left the door open to the genuine attack. *Mate in four moves* he thinks with satisfaction, as he too logs off.

He launches the Tor browser to take him back to the dark web, where he'll review the last contributions to his coding project. He scrutinizes the ordered lines of text and numbers across his two screens. Everything is in place.

Johns is in his forties now, and bitter experience has taught him not to trust companies to reimburse inventors fairly. Many believe the first industrial revolution proved that capitalism was the only viable system to achieve progress. He has a different view. The aims of business have become – have perhaps always been – a bid to exploit human labour. A game of subjecting the weak to its thrall, and sidestepping fair payment for an honest day's work. Its evil brother, compound interest, has even lured those who would otherwise have worked for the common good, to grasp for greater money-power. Johns is determined not to become their vassal.

As a professor of advanced surfaces at SouthWest University in Bristol, he has an aim: to establish a robust process for coating any material with a perfect diamond layer, at very low cost. He senses the imminent fulfilment of the experiments he's been conducting. The intellectual property of this diamond surfacing research will be priceless. The university has attracted huge sponsorship, including support from White Diamonds and several others. The race to achieve this is so intense that there is even a competing university nearby. They too have huge funding from White.

But Johns is a scientist, not a businessman. He felt badly hurt when corporate sponsors of a previous scientific breakthrough ruthlessly snatched it from him. They made a fortune from their 'relative addressable markets,' and he was left with a polite 'thank you'. Not this time. Johns calls the programme 'Domino' because sponsors love a title. Domino, a mathematical closed system, hints at the profound scientific challenges he's faced. He also likes the idea of dominoes placed on end, tumbling into infinity at the smallest of nudges.

Ironically, the turning point in his quest for security had been lunch with the urbane Clemens, a fellow professor, but of finance and investment. Money is not Johns' particular area of strength, as is clear to anyone who visits his shabby apartment. Though bookshelves line the walls, many of the titles stand in piles around the table at which he now crouches. It serves as a workstation, filing cabinet and somewhere to eat supper. If a vacuum cleaner were to mysteriously appear – unlikely as he neither possesses one nor believes in spontaneous manifestations outside of quantum mechanics – considerable effort would be necessary to ensure precious calculations were not consumed by it. A film of dust covers every surface. Johns only troubles this when he recovers a book from the murky and seldom-visited piles. An increasingly rare phenomenon. In short, Johns lives the life he assumed long ago; that of the mind. This leaves his body untroubled, unkempt and unloved. It was true that he'd inherited a cottage tucked away in a remote valley down in Cornwall, but this was the sum of his fortune.

Clemens is as smooth and sophisticated as Johns is earnest and gauche. Clemens enlightened his colleague on 'the sure way that money makes money,' by betting on currency. He explained how automated, high-speed trading makes millions of small-scale foreign exchange deals every minute. Of particular interest to Johns was the use of mathematical algorithms, that drive the sales and maximize profits for a trader. As someone who despises money-grubbing – perhaps because of his upbringing, perhaps his later student years in Moscow – he is not tempted personally. Not that he doesn't like money; he is as desperate for it as he is for love. In that way alone, he longs to be like the wealthy students, with their absurd confidence and pretty girlfriends. Even if he can't buy affection, he feels sure money will make him attractive.

Clemens' information had been exactly what he needed to unlock the power of the side-programme now on the screen. Some might call it malware ... but it is his insurance. Of course, this is off the books: carefully hidden from the university, sponsors of his research, and anyone who might use Domino in the future. It is present, nonetheless. *By all that is sacred in science, it is potent.*

The principle is simple. Johns has a formidable and brilliant mathematical mind, and he reveres elegance. He's based the malware on a combination of social cascade and availability bias. The more successful it is, the greater the volume of trades.

Domino's diamond-surfacing superpower will cause its owner to make a mountain of money. With the sub-programme in play, the reverse is guaranteed. Once activated, it assesses the stock market's concerns about the safety of certain investments. It will then calibrate the fluctuations in foreign exchanges worldwide. Finally, the malware trades stocks using automated currency transactions. The key is that the investment will be the opposite to that which common sense or wisdom would advise. Unless Johns disables the sub-programme, any party using Domino would simultaneously (and, most important, unknowingly) allow a back door into their bank accounts. Money would flow out and create massive exposures on the stock and currency markets. Like a giant, automated Ponzi scheme, the malware will financially annihilate the account holder. Fast.

Yes, this puts Johns in control until such a time as he has assurance that his work will be well compensated. He believes this is imminent.

5

TWO DEER

SAUL SPEAKS to no one on the way back to his desk. He sits there, eyes hard, staring and unseeing out of the window. *I can't do this.* He stuffs his laptop, his notebook and some papers into his soft leather shoulder bag, then takes the lift down to the garage, where his BMW motorbike rests. It gleams, in a shadowy niche, at the end of the long row of hefty, executive cars. He feels lucky that all the directors use four wheels and all of them German-made. *It fits right in.* The bicyclists have their racks in a separate, oversubscribed hangar. It apparently looked great on the architect's plans, but it's a maul at the end of each day.

The happy rumble of his exhaust, and the familiar pungent whiff of fuel, prompts a momentary, instinctive smile. Within minutes, he's on the road and moving swiftly towards the

Chiswick flyover, needing air in his lungs and the distraction of speed. The churning depths of his anger have returned. Passing the city limits, he opens the throttle of the powerful machine. Saul now knows where he's going. The motorbike cleaves through the humid summer air, with a rising excitement at being set free. He turns off the motorway eighty miles later, relaxing his speed to a respectable forty miles an hour, and easing onto a minor road. He is still clenching his teeth in fury. The deep green sights and smells of the Wiltshire countryside in mid-August come flooding through the closed visor. Finally, he cruises carefully up the short track that leads to the sturdy, broad, white-painted door at the back of the red-brick farmhouse.

The two-hundred-year-old homestead looks deceptively modest from this side. A long, two-storey mass, with just a window and back door visible, and with a one-up-one-down of a tiny cottage tacked on the end. Albie's office. But it's the short side of a long 'L', housing nine bedrooms, and with front and back gardens. Tall yew hedges guard the exterior, along with venerable climbing roses with stems as thick as a man's forearm. The main drawing room includes two fireplaces and French windows, opening onto the verandah and front lawn. This room alone is bigger than Saul's London flat. Worn quarry tiles have borne steps between the irregular levels of each downstairs room for generations. A faint, sweet smell of woodsmoke and wax polish permeates throughout. Saul grew up here. He feels the warmth of its occupants, both present and past. They're recorded in his bones, as much as in the stone and timber of the farmhouse.

He rocks the bike onto its stand, next to his brother's Range Rover, and unlatches his helmet, immediately smoothing his hair in the mirror. It's only then that Saul realizes how hot he's got in his bike leathers.

Xenia comes out to greet him, wreathed in smiles. 'This is an honour!'

Saul never had a sister so, when Albie married, he promptly appointed Xenia as a proxy. That she was slim, highly sensitive and with an impish smile was delightful. She wore her Nigerian-English parentage with ease, and had won the hearts and minds of the locals. As an artist, her creative disposition stopped Albie from getting fixed in his ways as a gentleman farmer. It also helped him communicate with his younger brother more skillfully. Better than the grunts of acknowledgement or the simple habit of pulling rank that he'd used when they were kids.

Xenia hugs Saul tightly. 'You're in luck; we've just got in.'

Albie appears by her side. 'I heard the bike. Come for coffee?' he asks, searching Saul's features.

Seeing the lines of tension, he says, 'No, a walk ... let me grab my binoculars.'

Saul smiles. 'I'll see you shortly, Zee.' He gratefully peels off his jacket and over-trousers, leaving them on the seat of the bike to air.

Albie reappears with a 'Coming?', and marches briskly off up the slope towards the cowsheds. Saul immediately catches up, and no sooner has he done so than his brother simply says, 'Shit?'

'Yes.'

'A woman?'

'No.'

'Work?'

Silence.

The brothers are a contrast in body shapes. Saul is slim, with a triangular face and sandy hair cut fashionably short. Albie is more corpulent and a couple of inches shorter, with a rounder face and wavy brown hair. Their genes ensured the same clearly defined facial features, straight-set eyebrows and high cheekbones. Both have the same peculiarly penetrating gaze.

Albie loves to walk out in nature. Preferably with a cigar in hand. Wherever he is, he regards it as his natural domain, and feels that it's his duty to enjoy life in whatever company he finds himself. He counts his blessings continually, in particular for his beloved Xenia. His brother comes a close second.

Saul, however, looks as any thrusting, young

investigative journalist should; his eyes seeking to cut out superfluous information. He keeps himself in shape out of healthy pride and less humble vanity, but also to manage the stress of his work. His urban life is in sharp contrast to Albie's. But if he has a true home, it's here and now.

They both know their conversation may be difficult. Their parents had left Albie the land. He was the elder brother and devoted to the farm. With it came both the responsibility and wealth to manage it.

Saul had excelled in other ways. He knows Albie feels bad that the division is so unequal between them.

'So?' asks Albie.

'It's my editor. Or if it's not her, it's the owners. Or maybe a DSMA notice.'

'Huh?'

'A government instruction to the media. It prevents us from sharing information about military and intelligence operations with the public. Allegedly, it's protecting the country.'

'Well, if it's the law, Saul ...'

'Someone wants it hushed up.'

'Can you tell me, or would you have to shoot me?'

'You're the one with the shotguns.'

'Yes, but I always wear tweed when I use them.'

Saul looks across at Albie's broad blue-and-white-striped, open-neck shirt and gives him a look.

'It's expected.'

'I've been working on this piece for over six months. It started two years ago with a handful of underwater mine attacks on ships and smaller boats in the UK overseas territories. It's no secret that it's escalated to include naval vessels around Britain and other countries. I'm convinced that a Russian company uses mercenary divers to plant limpet mines. They're hard to detect, and cause major damage at minimal cost.'

'Of course, I've read about the attacks. How do you know it's the Russians? What's your evidence?'

'Really?'

'OK, I get it, hotshot, but why?'

'The simple answer is: money. They have a unique anti-mine defence system.'

'So why not publish?'

'That, dear brother, is the multi-billion-dollar question. Did you know the UK is the second largest exporter of arms worldwide? Perhaps there's a big deal in the offing? Whatever, it's bullshit. I'm thinking of quitting the paper.'

'Ass.' Albie means it in the spirit of brotherly warmth, but immediately sees he's inadvertently pressed the big, red button marked 'DANGER'.

'It's easy for you to sit here with your nine hundred acres and charming wife and healthy animals and tell me I'm an idiot. What are you doing to protect democracy or honesty or free speech? Tell me that, Albie. If you don't have journalists to give you facts, where else will you get them from? Hollywood?'

Now it's his brother's turn to remain silent. They walk on, quickening their pace, as they stride along the causeway of a disused rail track that runs across the farm. Just then, Albie, staring straight ahead, places a large hand flat across Saul's chest. They freeze. Two red deer stand on the edge of a field ready for harvest, heads down, oblivious to the humans. Albie slowly passes his binoculars to Saul. The powerful lenses give a wonderful view of the gentle animals, enjoying a peaceful midday meal, in the warm English summer sunlight. It's impossible to feel agitated in the presence of these beautiful creatures.

Saul, ashamed of the bad temper in which he arrived, passes the field glasses back to his brother with a smile.

Albie winks.

'You'll stay, I hope?' asks Xenia.

'We've got him for at least a week,' replies Albie. 'Our man here has a big story to digest, so he needs a retreat.'

'I'm thinking about a change, Zee.'

'To what?'

'Everything.'

'Oh well, you'd better start by laying the table for lunch.'

'You wanted change!' said Albie. 'Be careful what you wish for!'

They laugh.

6

BLACK TIE

Conrad Harris smiles broadly, showing a lot of very white teeth. His narrow-set, blue eyes remain fixedly mean, below his thick crop of salt-and-pepper hair. He had graduated into politics, after a short career selling houses in Kensington and Chelsea. He knew that he couldn't live life as if in a goldfish bowl – fully visible to the public – without protection.

His remarkable rise towards the top of the political tree had been blessed from the moment the 'high net worths' adopted him. Professionally, he'd never had cause to regret it. The introduction had come several years previously, when Sergei Goryaev invited young Conrad Harris MP to attend the inaugural meeting of the UK-Russia Cultural Alliance. It was a gathering aimed solely at 'developing cultural and media relations'. Goryaev was a junior diplomat at the time, but already marked as a player. Conrad was just one of the twenty members of parliament present. The embassy entertained their guests lavishly and, from the first, any obstacle – certainly any obstacle requiring finance – had miraculously disappeared. This had facilitated Conrad's smooth ascent up the greasy pole of politics. No single event in his career had favoured him more. Nothing close.

One could say that it's improper to take money from those whose interests are not aligned with those of one's constituency or the country. But Conrad reassures himself that these are British citizens making the donation. *There's certainly nothing illegal about that, nothing at all. No, these are merely generous gifts from a handful of the two hundred ultra-wealthy Russians who requested, and received, a Tier One 'golden visa'. It's their right and their pleasure to invest in the UK. It's not for me to judge their morals. I don't have the figures, and frankly, it isn't my problem. This is merely democracy at work, whereby any British citizen can support the political party of their choice. I'm simply enabling them to do just that. Yes, I Conrad Harris, am a proud supporter of British democracy, and the devil take anyone who suggests otherwise.*

He doesn't choose to dwell further on the unpleasant truth that some political watchers decry such 'investments'.

Conrad is not naïve. He realizes that there are

dangers in 'a will not to know', as the fate of Lord Perisham demonstrated ... suspended from the House for helping companies with Russian connections that disliked inconvenient legislation. Conrad shivered at the thought that the Chief Whip must certainly have a file detailing his own indiscretions.

Anyway, Perisham is reinstated now, thought Conrad. He and his colleagues would ensure that the tenets of democracy are rigorously followed, especially in regard to accepting generous donations.

The only requirement of his current arrangement with Sergei (and it's certainly not an onerous one), is an informal meet-up once every three months. They would be at an event together, and thus naturally chat about items of mutual interest. They might touch on the cost of running a campaign for re-election, or other, extraordinary office expenses. The last such meeting had yielded fifty thousand pounds, but that was unusual. *Normally it's just a bit of fun: entertainment at a rugby international, a comfortable, fact-finding trip to a warm country. That sort of thing.*

Conrad is aware that six members of the Cabinet receive donations from the same source, either personally or via their constituency offices. Again, there's nothing more to say about this. *It's all legit and above board. Nothing to see.*

He helps himself and Sergei to another glass of

champagne. *My, these Russians can drink,* he thinks to himself. If the Right Honourable Conrad Harris MP feels anything other than sheer pleasure from the first three glasses, he certainly doesn't show it.

However, he has mentioned to Sergei that there are rumours about possible Russian mine attacks, and now his political antennae register that he's about to be asked a favour. He ascribes the faint perspiration breaking out over his temples to the warmth of the room. Conrad blames the tightness of his bow tie and the suffocating closeness of a tight waistcoat on too many lunches with generous lobby groups. He removes his jacket and feels the beads of sweat clinging under his arms. He puts them down to extra shoulder padding, rather than any sense he might be doing something improper.

Sergei regards him with a lopsided grin. *He's a charmer, this Sergei,* thinks Conrad.

'You think this is a good idea? For newspapers to talk about this?'

'Certainly not,' states Conrad firmly. 'No evidence, as far as I'm aware. Poking each other with sticks only hurts both sides.'

'Do you have some influence, my friend?' Sergei's smile is as broad as his mark's.

To Conrad, the dance music seems louder, but he smirks confidently and leans conspiratorially in towards his friend, to whisper, 'I don't think I need any. The media knows enough about DSMA standing notices not to jeopardize military operations or intelligence.'

'Might they need to be reminded?'

Sergei smiles with his eyes, which Conrad always finds very attractive. 'A chat with a couple of editors I know will do the trick. We're all trustees in a charity. Nothing heavy-handed. Just let them know we'd rather keep this quiet at present, yes? Perhaps promise to share information as soon as we have something definite?'

'It would certainly prevent any unpleasantness.'

Conrad and Sergei understand one another perfectly.

7

TROUBLE

Maxim Bovar is a very rich man, possessed of factories, banks and other great Russian enterprises. A huge, brash man, with a vehement stare and a metallic smile. A man made of brass, whom those of flesh and blood do well to avoid. Though possessed of a large body, his head is larger still, with swollen veins in his temples, and such strain in his face that his eyes are permanently half-shut. It gives him the appearance of being over-inflated and ready to explode. He resigned himself long ago to the loss of distinguishable bone structure in his face, but sees himself as good-looking ... in a manly way. A casual observer would – out of earshot – have used many words to describe him. But not handsome.

He is in his Moscow office and eases himself back into one of the four broad leather armchairs, in the sunken area, on the opposite side of the room from his desk. Large desks are so often used as an attempt to impress and impose on visitors. Bovar has other ways of doing that. His desk is oversize because a very large man needs a lot of room. It makes him feel normal, but not ordinary.

This is the problem of living in Moscow today: so many people, all of whom are bent on power. A word, a dismissive look, a bored yawn from the President, and a life could change. Seldom for the better.

But here, in the pool of natural light from the tall windows around him, all is calm. Here, he can lavish care on his beloved specimen orchids, glowing within their climate-controlled vivarium.

His wife sits opposite, showing her profile, so Bovar can admire her new nose, courtesy of some very expensive plastic surgery. Her beautiful and youthful appearance is remarkable, and he indulges the infinite pains she takes to sustain this. He is happy for his Tatiana to take her role as trophy wife very seriously, and to give her the freedom to become whatever she wants. As long as it's what he wants. For now, this requires she divide her time between sessions with her personal trainer, stylist and beauticians, with outings to lunches and charity receptions.

It was she who had suggested using compatriots in Britain. On the surface, an alliance with fellow business leaders (to further the glory of Mother Russia and, incidentally, magnify Maxim's own wealth), had seemed wise. He values his wife's native cunning in negotiation, but this also makes him cautious. He no longer hopes for love, but he does demand loyalty. His vindictive and faithless first wife had successfully deprived him of any contact with his children. By day, and surrounded by the busy-ness of his empire, he is invulnerable. But in the small hours of the morning, he can't hide from this pain. Now, all he asks for is to be recognized as a success by his country, and particularly by the President.

As one of the wealthier men in Russia, Bovar relies solely on trust and co-operation. And fear. To ensure this, he, like many of his friends, employs a private military company – a PMC – to enforce the proposals he makes to employees, competitors and suppliers. It rather suits him that this is a matter of public knowledge; in his experience, a little fear brings a lot of respect. Perhaps it isn't fair to think of Uri Bychkov and Vasily Vasiliev as mere suppliers; he admits a degree of shared destiny, but had baulked at the idea of partnership. Each of them has a business empire of his own. Like Bovar's, they had blossomed with a thousand flowers and substantial fruit, following the chaos of the USSR's political collapse in the 1990s. In one way they are true brothers-in-arms, but then, Bovar thinks, no brother would demand payment like this. Tatiana had advised it was unwise to use force, but it has since become a matter of control. If there is one thing at which Maxim Bovar excels, it is ensuring others follow his will.

'My dear, I have a tedious chore to complete: a call with our friends in the UK. I'll join you shortly.' He dismisses her with a smile that slides across his heavy face like a slick of oil over an expanse of dangerous water.

He notes that both Vasily Vasiliev and Uri Bychkov are already online, and puts the video call through via his private network to ensure security. They answer before the fifth ring. He has not enabled video at his end, to ensure that he maintains some small advantage.

'Tovarishch! It is so good to see your faces again.'

'We can't see you, Maxim,' says Vasily, one hand gesturing his exasperation.

British society has approved Vasiliev as an excellent man of business. He is as enterprising, vigorous and swashbuckling as the bright eyes, lean features and close-cropped bristle of prematurely silver hair on his round scalp suggests. His fingers are unusually short, suggesting a disposition to the practical, and even manual. Vasily Vasiliev is nothing if he is not pragmatic. He has a gleam for any material advance that favours him, but his style of executing business is not conducive to creating a happy world. He sees no profit in that.

'Ah, sadly, my laptop has no camera.' Bovar lied.

'Besides, I am old and ugly. Why would you want to see this face?'

'It is always good to see the face of a partner,' says Bychkov, his languid, patrician delivery clashing with the coarser tones of Bovar and Vasiliev. His voice is not affected by the pronounced hook of his nose, any more than his eyesight is affected by the closeness of his eyes to one another. He exudes disdain. Bychkov's aristocratic heritage, his aloofness and his modulation, mask the dark thoughts he habitually harbours. His thin smile is so intimidating that one would wish him to be merely scowling.

Before embarking on this relationship, Bovar had both the men checked out by Kalov, his head of security. It amazed him to read that Bychkov had, in his youth, trained as a tenor in the opera at the State Institute for Theatre Arts. *I will use that to my benefit one day,* he thinks with amusement.

'So true, so true.' Bovar continues. 'Next time. We have business to discuss. What is your proposal?'

'That is for you, Maxim,' said Vasiliev. 'We have fulfilled our side of the bargain. I trust this has been to your entire satisfaction.'

'Indeed. I also note we have avoided the attention of the press.' It amuses Bovar to distract them. 'An unexpected benefit.'

'That was Vasily's work. He appears to be an expert in the ways of influencing British media and politicians,' says Bychkov with unaccustomed generosity. The video accentuates the dark shadows around his hooded eyes. His air of superiority irks Bovar.

'It's remarkable what our embassy can achieve with nice dinners, and a few donations to campaign funds with our support,' chimes Vasiliev. 'That, and a good understanding of a politician's needs ...'

'Excellent,' responds Bovar. He enjoys the process of baiting Bychkov, and particularly Vasiliev. While the former had inherited wealth and slipped into the ownership of multiple factories with ease, Vasily Vasiliev had grafted to build his empire through legendary money-trading, as well as other, less well-publicized activities. He is much the more entrepreneurial of the two, but if anyone is to be feared in this conversation, it's Bychkov. He seems to care only for the standing of his family name.

'And I can trust in the absolute confidentiality of our arrangement?'

'Of course, Maxim, assuming you can settle this account satisfactorily,' says Vasiliev, with a note of irritation.

Bovar is not expecting either of them to take the initiative, but perhaps it's no surprise Vasily has stepped forward.

'You must understand,' he responds, 'the enterprise has not yet yielded profit.'

'The fact you haven't yet successfully sold your anti-mine defence system is not our problem,' replies

Vasiliev. 'We've used our mercenary assets at significant cost and reputational risk, to strike successfully at over a hundred targets. We have forced navies worldwide to recognize the huge value of a solution to limpet mines. You have an open market and, as far as we're aware, a monopoly. We've done our part, so now we expect to be paid.'

'What do you want?'

'We agreed a price, Maxim. If you don't have the cash, that's fine. We're happy to take diamond mines or financial services in lieu. We know you have both, besides your military supply interests, so it's your call. Perhaps you would advise us? By Monday.'

This confirms it for Bovar. The two are playing hardball to get their money. They've discussed this and have a plan. How dare they seek to impose on him?

'I merely wanted to confirm our arrangement,' he says smoothly, 'and will come back to you with a suggestion. Incidentally, the President has personally asked that I pass on his thanks. Goodbye, gentlemen.' With that, Maxim Bovar, head of Bovar Industries, and a good friend of the President himself, ends the call. Seething.

8

CERTIFIABLE

'A NEW RING, XENIA?' asks Saul, as he looks up from his colourful plate of salad. All meals are eaten at the old pine table in the kitchen, unless there's a particularly grand dinner party, when they'll use the dining room. There's even a hatch between the two rooms, vestigial from Victorian times, when the house had a cook and a handyman living in the cottage.

Albie picks absent-mindedly at his plate, perhaps searching for something meat-like which he hopes is hiding there somewhere.

Xenia blushes and waves the slim fingers of her left hand ostentatiously, so the fire of the diamonds flash beneath the kitchen down-lighters. 'Beautiful, isn't it?'

Saul takes her hand and studies the rock, surrounded by smaller stones which shimmer with the same white brilliance and fire as the centrepiece. 'That's some ring. Expensive, bro?'

Albie doesn't blush; it's not his style. 'Outrageous,' he says with an indulgent smile to Xenia, who is quick to intervene.

'Have you found a nice girl, Saul?'

'No time for that.' The small, dark look he gives, signals he hasn't yet moved on from his divorce the year before. The merest flicker of eyes between Albie and Xenia tells them that they need a change of conversation.

'Did you know, in ancient times, Indian fakirs prescribed a diamond strapped to an arm as a cure for sickness?' asks Xenia. 'They're meant to have both physical and spiritual healing properties. If you've got time this week, you should meet up with Albie's friend Ben. He's spent his entire life trading valuable gems, and has some fantastic stories.'

'Jewellery's an interesting business,' says Albie. 'Just pretty rocks, but we idiot humans spend a fortune on them. Zee and I visited a local company who claims it makes synthetic diamonds, but we wanted the real thing - and a certificate to prove it.'

'What do they mean by synthetic?' asks Saul.

'I can't really tell you, bro, but the Ferrers can. It's a husband and wife. Their schtick is around the ethical provenance of a stone made in a lab, rather than one dug up out of the ground. The people seemed OK. If you're serious about changing professions ... if ... perhaps they're worth a look. Imagine the number of pretty girls who like diamonds, real or fake. The diamonds I mean.'

Xenia gives her husband a pointed elbow jab in the ribs, and takes over. 'I looked into it, and there are a lot of so-called alternatives. We ended up with a dealer signed up to Fairtrade, so we knew the provenance of the centre stone we bought.'

'There are con artists around everywhere,' says Saul.

Albie studies the kitchen ceiling, muttering, 'Give me strength.'

Xenia continues, 'One person who is definitely the real thing, is my friend Polly. She's working on something to do with diamonds, so knows all about the science.'

'She's also extremely cute.' Albie grins. 'And coming here this weekend, as it happens.'

This time Xenia merely narrows her eyes at her husband. 'Your timing, Saul, is impeccable.'

Seeing a glimmer of enthusiasm in his brother, Albie asks, 'Shall I give the Ferrers a call to introduce you? Whilst I'm at it, let's connect you with Ben. Or you're welcome to help on the farm; we're mucking out the big cattle shed tomorrow.'

'So it's shit or diamonds?'

'You know what they say about muck ...'

9

PRESSURE

Bovar calls his head of security immediately after the conversation with Bychkov and Vasiliev.

He curses loudly, 'What will they try? Fucking fools,' unaware he's speaking out loud. 'I want them to know they don't mess with me. They think they can control this? We'll give them a message they won't forget.'

Ivan Kalov's brown, deep-set eyes and prominent cheekbones are the product of generations of suffering and endurance. Like a cliff facing the ocean, battered continuously by wind, the rain and the sea, his features retain only ridges and spurs. He stands stiff and erect, in his rigid uniform of black suit, white shirt, black tie and highly polished shoes; his hands hang loose by his sides and his long face rests mournfully. As ex-military and then foreign intelligence, he's trained in both patience and invisibility. He has seen too much to be moved by Bovar's rage, and knows he must let his boss vent.

It takes a further five minutes of swearing and beating of fists on the table – the water glass shaking with every strike on the massive desktop – before Bovar has calmed enough to listen to reason.

The imperturbable Kalov can now speak. The bass tones of his voice, firm and smooth, speak a volume of assurance. 'Sir, you talk of revenge, but are these not the same men who each has private military companies as well trained as your own? You chose them because their people can do things we cannot in overseas territories. Yes, your forces are strong, but they are high profile. You have always emphasized *maskirovka* ... we act in disguise.'

'I know this, Kalov. It's business: they've done what I've asked, and now I must pay. Fair enough. But they are arrogant.'

Kalov notes Bovar may be envious at the relatively politics-free careers of his chosen business partners, but is too wise to suggest this. 'We have honeytraps if you think they're withholding information.'

'No, they'll expect this. I want you to contract and prepare, but not yet deploy, squads to eliminate any threat from them. Do you hear me? I want final, ruthless removal of danger on my signal. They have crossed the line, and both their families and others must see that it does not do to antagonize me.

'They will surely have considered this? Your choice to use them was wise, as the actions cannot be attributed to you, your men, or even to Russia. We have total, plausible deniability.'

This massage of Bovar's ego seems to have the required result.

'I will pay them, but put the force into place, Kalov. That is all.'

10

KING OF DIAMONDS

Saul woke from a broken night's sleep, inhabited by strange dreams of unknown characters refracted in prisms of light. He set off for his meeting with the Ferrers, buoyed by the rush of oxygen from the sweet morning air, still cool, pouring through the visor as his bike bowled towards the outskirts of Salisbury.

As he entered the pillared opening of a modern, private estate, he felt a change of mood. He cruised slowly past both granite-faced houses, hewn from solid Victorian values, and modern brick-built homes. Each front lawn is immaculate. *Gated communities have an other-worldliness, and a curious intensity of their own,* thinks Saul. He is neither smug nor a hypocrite, and yet the conformity to an unwritten code makes his hackles rise. An image of a faded photo of his mother in hippy gear, obviously in her late teens, wells up in his imagination. Her favourite saying was 'Just living is not enough ... one must have sunshine, freedom and a little flower'. He smiles and makes a mental note to ask Albie if he still has that picture.

There are three cars in the Ferrers' drive, one of which is an ostentatious, white Mercedes. The garage door is open and, within, Saul sees the tangle of kids' bikes and paraphernalia typical of a suburban family. It's an unlikely venue for a revolution in the jewellery industry, but he'll keep an open mind.

As he dismounts, he glimpses Jeff Ferrers coming out to greet him. Saul keeps his back turned as he carefully removes his white full-face helmet, soft, cowhide summer gloves and leather jacket. He stows them neatly with the pair of matching trousers in the rear panniers. As always, he carefully smooths his hair in the reflection of one of the wing mirrors, and uses this to snatch a look at Jeff. Tall, muscular, grinning manically, and clenching his hands open and shut, open and shut.

Saul's experience as a journalist is that people are desperate either to publicize their business or avoid the glare of exposure. It's clear that Etique are in the first camp. As Saul turns, Jeff bounds forward and thrusts a meat plate of a hand towards him. 'Fantastic timing, man. The king of diamonds is here and he's mad to see our stones. Come on in.'

'Hi Jeff, good to meet you too. Who exactly is the king of diamonds?'

'Yeah, yeah. He's totally the main man. He's a world expert, and fascinated by what we're doing here,' yaps Jeff, already exhibiting signs of sickening over-enthusiasm, mixed with unbridled self-confidence.

The interior of the Ferrers' home is as spotlessly conventional as the exterior. Louise, like her husband, wears an open-neck shirt and jeans pressed with a crease but, thankfully, seems entirely sane. She greets Saul with a gentle handshake and looks directly at him with large eyes. Together, the couple look absurdly healthy, with glowing skin and shining hair, as though they've stepped directly out of a TV advert for a kitchen floor cleaner.

Together, they conduct him to the huge, airy kitchen, lit by a skylight and large windows, and duly introduce him to the 'king of diamonds'. He's a short, dapper, elderly jeweller, by the name of Carl Mason, dressed in a pristine tweed jacket, bow tie and lavender shirt. His half-moon spectacles dangle from a fine gold chain around his neck, and he smells strongly of cologne. Saul understands his business is Aurum, which has traded from 'humble premises' in Salisbury for the past thirty years. Carl wishes his 'son, also in the business, could be here too'. He is indeed 'intrigued by this so-called lab diamond'.

Once installed with coffee, at a long glass dining

table, the demonstration can begin. Jeff sits at the head with his two guests either side, and Louise opposite. Saul's notebook is open and ready.

'Everyone's talking about this, man.' If Jeff possesses the gene for British understatement, it is definitely recessive. Saul regards Louise and Carl, neither of whom seem to think this fountain of hyperbole is odd.

With a flourish, Jeff produces some A4 black-and-white images from a slim black leather briefcase. 'It's happening, man! This first picture shows the characteristic Raman spike of a diamond.' He nods vigorously as Carl and Saul examine the image. The paper is marked *Independent Lab Test, MIT; Spectroscopy*. It shows a simple two-line graph recording a comparison between the chemical properties of a 'natural diamond' and 'simulant'. In both, there's a pronounced spike in the same place.

'The signature of a real diamond, yeah?' says Jeff.

'I wasn't aware of that. Interesting,' replies Carl.

'Yeah!' says Jeff, with all the gusto of a delegate to an American sales conference. 'Now, these are images of our diamonds taken with an electron microscope.' Again, he shoves them across to Carl and Saul. Each image is captioned with a date, location, magnification used, and other, more arcane data. In its own way, it's moving to see the natural beauty of a stone's make-up at such high magnification. Together, the pictures show the unseen world of diamonds, and the signature square pyramidal forms of carbon crystals.

'OK, can you let me use your diamond pen, Carl?' says Jeff, then turning to Saul, 'This is a meter to test the authenticity of a diamond. If the row of LEDs light up to the DIA mark, it proves it's real, right, Carl?'

'That's correct, Jeff.' Saul now wonders if he's a watching a theatre double-act, but manages to keep a straight face. In what looks like a personal ritual, Carl raises his spectacles and positions them neatly on the end of his nose, with two hands. Saul notices his clean, neat hands, his manicured nails and unusually long eyelashes.

Jeff opens two small, brilliant-white paper packets with blue tissue interiors. Nestling within each are half a dozen cut stones of uniform size. 'Here are some of our highest-quality two-carat diamonds. Beautiful, aren't they? Do you want to inspect them first, Carl? Take three at random.'

With an elegant movement of his wrist, Carl draws a magnifying loupe from his waistcoat pocket and inspects a few stones with his expert eye. He separates three from the rest. 'These look well cut. I'd need a microscope of course, but ...'

'We leave the cut to the experts: we only use the best. Man, have we got a story for you guys! Wait until you see this,' says Jeff as he holds the tip of the diamond pen to one of the stones. The row of tiny LEDs light up. 'What does this mean, Carl?'

The older man pauses, moistening his lips, his brow furrowing as he looks at Jeff over the top of his glasses. 'This is a diamond. No doubt about it.'

Jeff repeats the action with the remaining two stones, each time showing Saul the LEDs as they pass the threshold.

'Are these pens expensive?' asks Saul.

'They're very reliable,' replies the jeweller.

'OK, so now I'm going to blow your mind,' says Jeff, barely able to contain himself. Louise, meanwhile, sits at the far end of the table, composed and barely listening, it seems. She glances occasionally at Saul, then Carl, and then her husband, but says nothing.

'Cutting to the chase, Jeff, is this for real?' asks Saul. 'I've read about lab diamonds, but understood they're very inferior.'

'I've shown you. I've shown him, Carl, haven't I? You've seen it now. Do you believe your eyes?'

'I can't deny the evidence,' answers Carl. 'You used my diamond pen. I know it functions perfectly and can thus distinguish a false from a real stone. These are undeniably high-quality authentic diamonds. Is this Raman spike and these other images from your stones? And you say they're simulants? Is that the same as synthetic?'

'We don't like to call them 'synthetic', Carl. No,

these are real diamonds, created in the laboratory. I'm a trained scientist. This is a world first. These are incredible.'

'Jeff,' Saul asks, 'where are they made? You don't make them, right?' He bites his tongue, as he notices he's using Jeff's speech pattern.

'No, man. No.' Jeff is once again grinning wildly, like a demented cartoon monkey. 'They're made for us by a super high-tech facility in China.'

'Exclusively?' asks Carl.

'Exclusively,' says Louise. The first words she's spoken since they sat down. Saul pivots in his seat to look directly at her, and she looks directly back, wide-eyed and smiling, her white teeth exposed. 'Exclusively.'

'So what's the catch?' says Saul. 'Why haven't I heard of this before? If this is a commercial proposition – which I gather it is, as I've seen your website and talked to a customer – this is a game changer. Why isn't it well known?'

'They don't want it out there,' said Louise.

'Who are *they*?'

'White Diamonds,' she replies, glancing at their other guest for confirmation. 'Carl's on the jewellery advisory council to White Diamonds. You tell him, Carl.'

There's a long pause as the older man looks over his half-rim spectacles, appraising Saul. 'White Diamonds are a very well-established company – you know them, of course – and supply, by a large degree, the majority of stones to the jewellery industry. At one time it was a global monopoly, and some claim it remains so, hidden behind complex ownership structures. They employ many, many people worldwide, and continue to invest heavily in mining. I can see they would not be happy to have diamonds ... manufactured.' Even Carl, it seems, has a slight distaste for this new process. 'People might assume these new stones are of equal value to those won by, ah, traditional means.'

'Would you sell these stones?' asks Saul.

'We don't sell stones, we sell jewellery.'

Louise cuts in, smiling at Carl. 'Speaking as a woman, jewellery is a beautiful expression of love. It's a great way to remember the most important moments in life.'

The jeweller smiles warmly in return. 'Yes, indeed, it's proven to be an enduring way to celebrate all of life's great events: engagement, marriage, birth, anniversaries. Diamonds are timeless.'

Saul feels the conversation slipping away into marketing-speak. 'But the bottom line is that a lab-created diamond, 'a simulant', 'a synthetic' or whatever, is valuable?'

'It's a diamond. Right on.' Jeff smiles beatifically.

'What's more, it's entirely ethical, which is why we call our company Etique,' says Louise.

'If I bought one, would I get a certificate proving it's a diamond?' Saul thinks he senses unease in the room at his question. Interesting.

'Today, that's a problem,' says Jeff. 'The issue is not the stone. No. The problem is that White Diamonds run the industry. As White don't want these recognized as real diamonds, they won't allow their system to certify them. So, while these are the real thing, they're rejected on the grounds of very slightly different trace minerals from those found in mines.'

Saul looks at Carl for confirmation, but can read nothing there. 'So we've got a scientifically true diamond, an industry controlled by a major supplier, and millions of willing buyers, is that right?'

'You bet,' yaps Jeff. 'People fall off their chairs when they hear the cost.'

'I'm guessing it's cheaper.'

'Here's the kicker: one quarter of the price.'

'You offer the same weight and quality of stone for a quarter of the price of a mined diamond?' asks Carl, whose eyes seem to have expanded like a small child being offered unlimited ice cream.

'You bet, daddy-o.' Jeff looks like he's about to high-five the jeweller, but holds back at the last moment. Instead, he quivers like an oversize tuning fork, eyes staring in wild excitement at his guests. 'Whaddya ya think, Saul?'

What Saul thinks is that this sounds too good to

be true. What he feels is different. Despite his journalistic scepticism, bordering cynicism, his instincts are saying, *This is it! This is bloody well it.*

'It really is that good, Saul,' says Louise, again training her large eyes on him.

He feels he's impervious to a woman's charm after the savage end to his marriage, but this business looks like an amazing opportunity. He puts down his pen and checks his notes to confirm what he's now thinking: *this could make my fortune*. He also feels, like a physical pressure, the pain of rejection in his work, the betrayal of the values it represents, and the inequity of wealth between him and Albie.

'What do you need?' he asks.

Louise and Jeff exchange a look. Carl looks quizzical.

'That depends on what Carl needs. Can you sell this, Carl?' says Louise.

The jeweller looks back at his hostess with the warmest of smiles. 'You know I'd love to, Louise, I really would. I can't stick my neck out. My son, perhaps? The industry is changing and I want him to take the business over. He too must work with White Diamonds and ...' His voice trails off. 'You will take so much business from traditional jewellers. Diamond merchants will see you as a threat, Louise.'

'Of course, Carl, we understand.' Louise turns to Saul. 'You see, initially we must sell direct to the public. To do that we need you to tell people about it.'

'You need a marketing agency, perhaps?' asks Saul.

'After you called to set up this meeting,' Louise says, 'we did some research. You're respected and very well connected. We think you'd be great to work with. Not just an article, but as part of Etique. We want you to join us.'

'I know nothing about jewellery or diamonds or anything like that. I'm just a reporter.'

'But you could do something on the side to begin with, perhaps? This is a very lucrative business. Very.'

'We pulled down over half a mill last year, Saul,' says Jeff. 'And we weren't even trying. That was Louise on her own. This is our time. We're ready, man.'

11

BREAKTHROUGH

The Materials Research building is a twenty-minute cycle ride from Johns' apartment. The anodyne three-storey structure, with its dully reflective windows, looks blankly over a pleasant residential road. For a university town, it's not out of place. Johns feels buoyed by the warm summer sunshine, as he pedals past the line of cherry trees that lost their blossom months ago. He padlocks his bicycle to the railings and releases his briefcase from the two restraining bungee cords. He is in a world of his own, taking quiet pleasure in knowing the coding for his insurance scheme is complete.

He walks swiftly to his office on the second floor, barely registering the familiar sulphurous, chemical odour pervading the corridors. It's an inevitable consequence of the gases used here. He drops his case by the desk, removes his jacket and goes next door to the lab, without donning a white coat. He just wants to show his face and see his assistants. One in particular.

While Johns is serious to the point of distraction about his work, the demand on scientific knowledge in this phase of the research is not great. The operations require rigorous methodology, and careful recording, that is all. For this reason, he allows himself the indulgence of choosing lab technicians based simply on competence, reliability and physical good looks. They are female, and under thirty. He reasons that, as his genius requires elevation, it's only sensible to have people around who inspire him. Polly being his favourite.

As he enters the tall, white room, Johns feels reassured by the courses of shining stainless steel pipework feeding the expensive, matt-grey cabinets, surrounded by workstations. This is the state-of-the-art chemical vapour deposition foundry, in which they hope to forge a modern miracle of micro-engineering: the perfect diamond layer. Other teams have developed ways to create thin layers of carbon, but the process is slow, expensive, and the result is often unsatisfactory. A small fault makes all the difference. The existing diamond-like coatings are just temporary barriers at best, and unable to endure stresses or impacts.

A pure layer of carbon, four atoms deep, can withstand a round from an AK47 machine gun.

Johns' work is therefore of interest to the military, who are so excited by the potential for special surfaces, they've over-excitedly dubbed it 'Superman tech'. *If I am successful – when I am,* he corrects himself – *the breakthrough will mark the beginning of a new age for electronics, for optics, for molecular assembly, and for every stable surface.* It's what he's been searching for his entire working life, and he and his team are close. Very. More than that, their work aspires to produce faultless diamond surfacing, at high volume and nominal additional cost.

The expectations of the university's powerful, commercial partners are huge, and their potential profits limitless. It was no surprise that they'd signed off on the installation of this new equipment, at vast extra expense. As the college didn't have room to store the old gear, Johns had generously offered to keep it at his bolthole in Cornwall for 'further research purposes'. The university was enthusiastic, and even paid the manufacturers to transport and commission it in the far south-west where it now sat ready, in an outbuilding. Johns himself had borne the cost of installing a large diesel generator for power.

Polly is standing at an electron microscope, studying samples from the latest production run. Her short gold-blonde hair shines in the morning light, her fringe just visible in profile. She smiles as she turns her sapphire-blue eyes on him. Johns admires her pale, radiant skin, and feels elevated by her shining self-confidence.

'Good morning, Polly. Good morning, Lucy, Anna.' He nods at each in succession, noting they are all wearing regulation yellow lab gloves, and the collars up on their white coats. Each smiles back easily.

'Is all in order? What gas are we running today?'

'Boron today, Professor.'

'Anything interesting in the results from the overnight test?'

'You should see for yourself, Professor.'

Johns likes this bit the most. Polly always smells so clean when he comes close to her. He's pleased he used aftershave this morning. He peers through the eyepieces, blinks and lifts his head to look at her. He lowers it again and lets out a long, low breath. His mind begins to race. 'What is this?'

'Carbon nanotubes, sample 1394f, multilayer, nitrogen, copper seeds.'

'From our foundry? Here? Last night?'

'Yes, Professor.'

'I can see no imperfections. Please give me a reading of the set-up.'

Polly hands him a print-out. He scans it scrupulously, then looks again through the microscope. 'Pass me samples *e* and *g*, Polly.' He inspects these with as much care as the other. 'Ladies, please gather round. Together, we have achieved a world first.' He waves at the microscope, 'Take a look at perfect diamond surfacing.'

As they each examine the sample, the next steps become luminously clear in Johns' mind.

'No one is to say a word to anyone outside the lab about this. We have to confirm our results through multiple tests, in the strictest confidence. Is that clear? We also have to test the adhesion properties both to itself and to other materials.' Three smiling faces give him the answer he needs. 'Please set the foundry to repeat the same process as the one we ran last night. We can review the results together at the end of the day. Congratulations, team.' With that, Johns retires to his office, with his mind buzzing at the possibilities, demands and responsibilities of the news.

Eight hours later, the team are once again assembled in the lab, the initial results confirmed and a further run initiated. Now, the atmosphere is festive. They all know the value of the experiments.

'We have to celebrate,' says Polly.

'Yes, of course,' says Johns. 'What do you suggest?'

'If we can't talk to anyone, that leaves the four of us. Let's start with drinks and go on from there.'

'Ah, you go, I don't drink,' says Johns.

'You have to make an exception tonight, so that's that,' says Polly.

The blue dash of her eyes thrills him more than he dare admit, and he nods helplessly in agreement.

Three hours and several drinks later, the room is spinning. His colleagues have proven their considerable prowess with alcohol, and seem perfectly capable of holding a conversation without him. Johns knows he can't consume any more, but is drunk-confident enough to do one thing first. He leans towards Polly, trying to focus on her face but looking at her chest. With the absence of a lab coat it seems remarkably free of clothing.

'Polly, I need to go home,' he says unsteadily.

'Professor! We've only just started.'

'No. You're wonderful. I need to go home now, but something ... something occurs to me.'

'OK.'

'You should come too.'

'You need help to get home? If you really must leave, we can drop you off on the way to the restaurant.'

'No, I want you ... to come home with me ...'

Polly laughs with all the gaiety of youth and freedom. She affects a Texan accent. 'Oh, but Professor, you haven't made me a diamond yet.'

'But I could, couldn't I?'

There's a momentary flicker of disdain, or something worse, before Polly smiles sympathetically, placing a hand on his cheek. She turns to the others. 'We've got to drop the prof at home on the way. Let's go, girls.' And the three handsome young female scientists help Professor Johns up from the banquette. They half-carry him out to the warm summer evening air and pour him into a cab that's only just discharged its occupants.

12

MAVERICK

Twenty-four hours after his visit to Etique, Saul pulls up on a rutted track, lined with dense hedges, on a green hillside in the middle of nowhere. After the call to Ben Seiter, and with a small smile, Albie had passed Saul a scrap of paper with a mobile number and the words 'simple.fun.fish'. He enjoyed playing games with his brother, and was disappointed when Saul understood the reference.

He removes his earplugs, and all he can hear is the riffle of the hedgerows, in a soft breeze, carrying the scent of wild flowers and ripe wheat, and swallows darting overhead with a thin, high peep. Up here, in this moment, he feels the abundance of nature as though it were the very blood in his veins.

He checks the map to confirm he's in the right place, then dials the mobile number. *At least the signal is good up here.*

'Ben? Saul here.'

'I'll come and get you. Give me five.'

That means ten, thinks Saul. He strips off his bike gear and leans on the seat, as the sun beats down in an uncharacteristic display of summer friendliness. He smooths his hair carefully into shape, then reflects on what he'd be doing if he'd stayed at work. In an office, on a plane, alone in an hotel room, in a cab. He loved the surges of insight from research, an occasional flash of comprehension, and the craft of expressing himself precisely in the written word. But the rest of it ...

Forty-eight hours before, Saul had still considered himself a crusader. Leaving university at twenty-one, he'd joined the newspaper, and twelve years later felt he'd gone as far as he was going to go. Back in the heady days – just after his degree – the world seemed open, immense and generous. He'd consciously abjured commercial life, despite the initial pressure from his peers and his father. He'd wanted to make a difference, and a serious national newspaper looked like the best way to influence both society and decision-makers. That was then. The rejection of his most recent story had cut him hard and deep; the bitter pain of it seemed to be growing. Now his mind was illuminated by a new possibility: could he change the world and make money at the same time? Diamond mining had a bad reputation both for using slave labour and damaging the local ecosystem. If Etique were right, a lab diamond would be a social and environmental revolution. It would also be a fantastic money-making opportunity. He had to find out more.

'Saul! Over here.' A figure is looking at him through a hole in the hedge. Saul checks his watch: exactly five minutes.

'Good, you didn't spot the gap.' Ben speaks quickly, but the tone is unmistakably German and privately schooled. His frame is spare and almost bird-like, with a lined and weather-beaten face; his deep-set eyes, beneath a multi-coloured, woollen skull cap, glint with ferocity and vigour. He's unlike anyone Saul has dealt with in his urban life.

The two men weave back through the hedge, and stride to the top of a slope. A short way below, wholly obscured from the track up which Saul had driven, is an old showman's caravan, in dark wood, with cut-glass crystal windows. Beyond is a large, cream pyramidal tent and two smaller ones, each sky-blue. If they weren't exquisitely kept and precisely ordered, the ensemble would have looked like a hippy encampment. It didn't. Ben waves him into the largest tent, furnished with single classical statue on a pedestal, cushions and a low table.

'You know it? A resin copy, and smaller of course,' Ben says. 'Too heavy otherwise. The Winged Victory of Samothrace. I'll get the tea.'

Saul quickly learns Ben is not a man of mild

opinions. He's made a fortune buying and selling gems around the world, and eventually hung up his travelling boots to live a simple life on his own terms.

'I don't trust The Establishment in any way. I have a mobile, yes, but live off-grid. I only trade cyber now,' he states.

'Bitcoin?'

'Whatever. But that's not why you're here, is it? Diamonds.'

'Yes,' said Saul, refreshed by Ben's candour.

'We begin at the beginning. Diamonds are scarce, right? No. I've got a twenty-carat stone round here somewhere. Now that's rare; I'll dig it out for you later. Worldwide production of cut stones is around fifty million carats. Fifty million ... yes, put that in your pipe and smoke it.'

Saul smiles at the English idiom delivered in a German accent.

Ben continues, 'What if I tell you fewer than one per cent of mined diamonds,' he pauses for dramatic effect, both index fingers in the air to demonstrate quote marks, 'are responsibly sourced? There are very many people who know this but few who admit it. So, the question is: how to identify that one per cent.?'

'Surely there are safeguards ... ?'

'You've heard of the Kimberly Process, perhaps? This was set up to tackle blood diamonds. For instance, the war in Congo – largely financed by diamond wealth – killed five million people between 1998 and 2003. Eighty per cent. of their mined gems are traded illegally in the capital Kinshasa. You can see the same scheme in Angola, Ivory Coast, Sierra Leone, Liberia and many more. International agreements are made by Evian-sipping ladies and gentlemen in air-conditioned boardrooms, but the market is on the street.'

'So the system isn't working?'

Ben pauses to check his guest is merely being ironic, 'We say, *Da haben wir den Salat* ... it's all a mess. Ninety per cent of the world's mined diamond output travels to Surat in India as either a legitimate shipment, or smuggled in the guts of a human mule. The stones are processed, sorted, mixed and mixed again before travelling on to the world's largest diamond trading exchange in Mumbai. By this point, any trace of a diamond's origin has long since been cut and polished away.'

'But the legit ones still have a certificate, right?'

'A Kimberley Process document requires only the boxed weight of a consignment, its country of origin, and the importer-exporter. Legit and dirty stones are easily mixed without adjusting the certificate. The refreshed consignment may include just one single diamond from the original batch.'

'I don't understand.' Saul's mind whirls with the new reality presented to him.

'I'll keep it simple. When rough diamonds are

cut and polished, they lose fifty per cent. of their original weight. Ballast, in the form of conflict diamonds, is added to make the scales balance with the paperwork. So, the Kimberly Process is now a smokescreen for blood diamonds. It gives the industry a cover story to continue in the way it always has. It's like travel papers for a bag of stones, but it's only the bag that has the passport. The consignment changes.'

'Don't the police monitor this? Isn't it someone's job to give it teeth?'

'Stones seized by customs are auctioned to the public on a government website. They then magically become legal. Like many things, it may be lawful, but it's not ethical.'

Ben picks up his tea and gazes into its steaming surface, as through scrying a crystal ball, then turns to a newspaper clipping. 'The Kimberley Process was introduced to end the trade of rocks for rockets. It's become a convenient veneer. Official papers that bless black market stones with the halo of authority. Even the *Times of India* reports that more than one third of mined diamonds are smuggled illegally.' He tosses the cutting into Saul's lap. 'And we haven't begun to talk about what 'responsibly sourced' actually means.'

'Holy shit. So there really is a problem with the ethics of the diamond industry?'

'It's laughable, and we haven't yet touched on forgeries and the trade in certificates. I always worked outside the system. Just born like that, I suppose. I bought the stones from interesting people, and sold them to those that wanted them. I like to avoid trouble, but found it often enough.'

Saul had been sitting on a thin cushion, entirely upright, but something about Ben's candour causes him to relax, to give up the pretence of social correctness, and simply be himself. He pulls three cushions behind him, and leans back, gazing up at the interior peak of the tent. Was he a reporter digging for a story? He'd found it. Was he an entrepreneur looking for an opportunity? He'd found that too.

His host continues, 'India was a great place to do business. My favourite dealer was in Bombay. I'd visit his small, dark room, lit by a single, small desk lamp, the walls entirely covered by tiny drawers, each of which cradled a treasure. Remarkable times. No more. Now it's all industrial parks and permits and customs duty. Different clothes, same business.'

Saul reflects on the conversation with Etique, and how Ben's life, as a gem trader, was as much driven by the romance of the encounters, and the beauty of stones, as it was mercantile. 'Do you think it's a good business?' he says, as he sits up to look his host in the eye.

'It was never a good business, Saul. It was a great way of life. I've been lucky: I had fun, and made some money.'

'How can I tell whether a diamond is real?'

'White Diamonds have a purpose-built fortress on the Isle of Man. It has nine storeys underground. The lowest level is one large chamber filled with wheeled bins, just like you put out on the street for a rubbish collection. Every one of those containers – every single one – is full of diamonds. A diamond and its rarity is all as real as you believe it is.'

'I don't understand. Again!'

Ben laughs. 'As I see it, you're asking me about getting into the game. I'm telling you it's full, with one player holding all the cards.'

'But if someone else came along with a brand new pack of cards?'

There is a moment's silence.

'People have money. They like pretty things. You can sell them anything if they believe in it, and that's how White Diamonds came to be so strong. They created a myth and people bought into it. If you've got a good enough story and can get people to listen ...'

'But what about machine-testing of stones and modern certificates?'

'It's all bullshit, Saul. So, a piece of paper tells me it's a diamond? As far as I'm concerned, this is about trust. If I believe in the person who's selling to me, I'm happy. I don't trust anyone in that business anymore.'

13

NOT QUITE RIGHT

It takes just half an hour to travel from the primitive idyll of Ben's hedgerow to the suburban flatland of Etique; from the nodding of wild flowers in the meadows, to the strict ranks of roses in the front gardens, via the warm-throated gurgle of his exhaust pipes. To Saul, it feels like the journey from a distant colonial past to a technocratic future.

His rage towards *The Inquirer*, the fury and hurt over the end of his marriage a year ago, and the fear of letting go of his established career have amalgamated. He's ready for a new start, pushed by events as much as pulled.

He'd first learnt about the manufacturing of diamond simulants whilst researching Maxim Bovar's business interests. As these weren't directly related to the mine attacks, he'd mentally filed them under 'other'. His conversation with Ben, and the research into synthetics he did last night, have fanned the flame of his desire.

Once again, he rolls his bike onto the pristine driveway. He takes all the time he needs to dismount, stow his gear and revive his hair, before ringing the bell.

Louise opens the door. 'We didn't expect to see you so soon,' she says. Saul can see something is wrong. Her face is drawn.

'I'm sorry to drop by unannounced. I want to check some information.'

'Jeff's not here. I'm alone.'

'I can come back later.'

She pauses, then the tension around her eyes and mouth vanish as though a burden were lifted. She smiles radiantly, 'No, come in. Jeff will be here soon.'

Louise installs Saul at the kitchen table and brings him coffee.

'It's great you're keen. We've worked so hard on this, but know we need help.' Again, she smiles warmly at Saul, showing her perfect white teeth.

The sound of the front door opening heralds Jeff's arrival.

'Honey?'

'In here. Saul's dropped by.'

Jeff sweeps in, briefcase in hand. 'I saw the bike.' His grinning face as fixed as ever. 'You're back. That's great!'

Saul smiles politely.

While Jeff makes coffee and Louise cuts up fresh fruit, their banter seems entirely normal. *All very civilized,* thinks Saul, as he consults his notebook in preparation for the chat.

'Before we continue, and so I can tell you everything you want to know, would you sign this short non-disclosure agreement?' says Jeff. 'It simply ensures our trade secrets remain, er, secret!'

The one-page document looks straightforward, and Saul signs and dates it. He needs a solid foundation for the decision he wants to make. 'I'm going to come straight to the point,' he says. 'I want to check my understanding, so please be patient. I'm only after the facts.'

'Sure, sure.' Jeff nods.

'The stones I saw on Wednesday: they're a true diamond, is that correct?' Saul watches Jeff intently.

He flinches. 'Entirely.'

'Which is to say they're created in laboratory conditions – in China, I understand – in a revolutionary process that results in a first-class diamond, give or take a few trace elements?'

'Yes.' This time Jeff stares straight back. Either he's telling the truth, or is an experienced liar.

'Who's making them?'

'What do you mean?'

'I mean who, specifically, is producing these stones?'

'Ah. OK, so you've signed the NDA. I can tell

you. It's a genius university professor in China, working on laser systems for rockets, where they use the same material for lenses.'

'So there's a defence angle?' enquired Saul.

'No-no-no-no. No. He's a scientist like me. I trained as a scientist. This is inorganic, non-metallic carbide material. You're thinking of defence technology. He doesn't do anything like that. He's just come up with this idea of making diamond for lenses, and wants us to sell them.'

'And the stones have all the same qualities as a mined diamond, but without the considerations of forced labour, conflict stones, environmental damage and other ethical concerns?'

Jeff smiles broadly, showing excellent dental care. 'That's it, Saul. Awesome, eh?'

'And how are the stones made? Are they HPHT, or CVD, or something else?'

Jeff looks less self-assured for a moment, then resets himself. He's a tall man and leans back in his chair, arms across his broad chest. For some reason that Saul can't place, he looks more threatening. 'I can see you've done your homework. It's carbon vapour deposition. CVD.'

'And they're cut and polished in China?'

'Let me show you something.' Jeff produces his smartphone which, Saul notes, only became available in the UK a week ago. He hands it over as it plays a video of a workshop with rows of Chinese women – some of them very young – cutting and polishing sparkling gems.

'Our factory in China.'

Saul glances at Louise. Poker face.

'OK. So how come Etique – out of the entire global population of companies – gets to market this product? I don't understand.'

'Oh, that's really easy to answer. I found him.'

'You found the only guy in the world who makes lab diamonds?' Another miniscule movement from Jeff. Saul checks Louise's reaction. It hits him now. *They're hiding something.* All the warning signs are there. 'If we're going to work together on this, Jeff, I need totally reliable information.'

'What do you need to know? I'm open.'

'Are the stones a hundred per cent diamond, or are they coated? I've read that CVD technology can surface any material and,' Saul checks his notes for confirmation 'that a diamond layer bonds well to carbon substrate. For instance, silicon carbide; also known as carborundum or moissanite.'

'You've seen the graph: the Ramen spike.'

'I know what you've shown me, but I need you to answer my question.'

Jeff smiles broadly, 'The diamond pen tells you all you need to know.'

'It tells me what's on the surface, but it doesn't tell me about the heart of the stone.'

Jeff's lower lip begins to quiver. Fear engulfs his

features, momentarily revealing a man riven with self-doubt. An internal battle evidently takes place, as Jeff fights against a whirlpool of emotions. He re-asserts his will, and glares iron-faced at Saul.

'You're calling me a liar.'

'Certainly not.' Saul knows this gambit all too well. He senses the two opposing currents within him: one is the familiar shiver of a story unfolding, the other is the dark abyss of disappointment yawning below, as though he were at the edge of a precipice.

'How dare you call me a liar, this is my house.'

'I just want to know what's being sold here.'

'Keep out of this.' Jeff then turns his stare across the table to Louise. 'You put him up to this. You want me out of the company!'

Saul now understands the trepidation he felt earlier.

Jeff explodes, 'You two are in it together. I get it.'

'I'm not *in* anything, Jeff,' says Saul. 'You invited me to get involved.'

'Who are you to poke your nose in here? You're a hack, who makes trouble, and then publishes it in some shit newspaper. Get the fuck out of my house.'

'Answer Saul's question about the stones, Jeff.' It's Louise. Saul turns. She's far from inscrutable now, and stares manically at her husband.

'Oh, yeah. You want me to go there? OK. Saul, the stones my wife sells are fakes. Every damn one of them. I get them made up in China, lovely cut, and yes, silicon carbide: harder than diamonds. I get my man to spray them with a diamond glaze and hey presto! It's what people want. Of course, they're not the real thing, but Louise is really good at fooling the punters, particularly the men, aren't you, baby?'

'I didn't know they were fakes.' says Louise through pursed lips, eyes hard. 'You told me they were real.'

'You know exactly what you're selling, and you know how much profit we make on each stone. How could I get real diamonds for a tenth of the market price? Even a lousy reporter wasn't going to swallow that.'

Saul now stands, breathing deeply, watching the charade unfolding in front of him. He ignores Jeff's insults and moves towards the kitchen door, in a bid for freedom.

'Don't go, Saul.' It's Louise.

Jeff turns to Saul with a sneer, 'You're better off out of it, my man. She's a nightmare.'

Saul heads towards the front door and hears Jeff say to Louise, 'So what are you playing at?'

He lets himself out of the house, leaving the shouting match behind him. He puts on his helmet and gloves, turns the engine over, rolls back off the driveway and sets off at a brisk pace. His hopes for business success evaporating as quickly as they appeared.

14

MAKE ME AN OFFER

Johns fumbles so badly with the key that Polly has to offer to do it for him.

'No, no, the lock sticks,' he lies. Then, as the door swings open with alarming speed, he swivels his head and says, 'Are you sure you don't want to come in?' He attempts a charming smile, but his facial muscles refuse to respond, resulting in something between a grimace and a leer.

'Good night, Professor,' says Polly, and skips down the five steps to the pavement and the safety of her colleagues.

Johns goes directly to his desk and sits heavily down. Every part of his body feels weighted. The soft evening light floods the room comfortingly and seems to mock his troubled mind. Purely out of mechanical habit, he lifts the lid on his laptop and sees a prompt from the chess website: Loge has played.

I must snap out of this. He frowns at the clever move to block his feint. *Old fox, you're not so smart today,* he says to himself, and immediately puts his own queen into play. Only then does he realize his mistake, and checks whether Loge is online to see it. He is. A chat message immediately comes in.

Are you OK?

It dawns on Johns that he needs to lie down. The room is moving around him. *Of course,* he replies. Perhaps Loge won't notice his error.

You're sacrificing your queen?

He has. Johns doesn't make mistakes. Neither in science nor in chess ... at least not until now.

Do you need to speak, my friend?

Johns thinks talking is overrated but, today, with his professional star in the ascendant and his romantic dreams at their nadir, he very much wants to talk. After all, they've spoken previously to discuss games, or to extend a scientific topic they'd established of mutual interest.

Skype?

Two minutes later, audio is established.

'That was very unlike you.' Loge's thick, steady Russian tones seem surreal, coming after the raucous chatter of the bar, in which Johns had spent the evening.

'Yes,' admits Johns, with a long sigh. 'It's been a very exciting day.'

Loge can hear the slurred tones and waits.

'We've had a breakthrough.'

'Congratulations.'

'Bloody wonderful. We've done it.'

'What have you done?'

Johns remembers his code of silence. But this is different. Loge is his friend. He is a fellow scientist and will understand. 'In the lab.'

'Ah, your layering?'

Johns is confused that Loge knows, but thinks perhaps he must have told him previously.

'Yes, perfect.'

'And perhaps you are celebrating?'

'Yes, the girls wanted to drink. I don't drink.'

'Neither do I. Very wise.'

'But I did.'

'Ah. I wanted to check you are OK. We'll play again tomorrow? Goodnight, my friend.'

Johns' work had always made him a person of interest to Loge. He regrets having to compromise their friendship, but as chief technology officer for Maxim Bovar, it's now inevitable. It's past 11 p.m. in St Petersburg, and Loge is already tired. He doesn't like to do this to a fellow scientist, but it's his job.

Loge puts a call in to Bovar and the industrialist picks up immediately.

'Loge, you realize your employer sleeps at night?'

'Yes, sir. One of my targets has delivered in England. They have a breakthrough of priceless value to our military and consumer divisions.'

'Tell me.'

'Diamond surfacing.'

'Remind me.' Bovar's inability to grasp the wonder of this material causes Loge, once again, to regret he is tied to working with someone as stupid as he was rich.

'Super-strong, super-hard, super-light. Universal applications. Globally important.'

'Yes, yes, I know it's good for military use,' Bovar does not like to lose face in front of employees, no matter how clever they are, 'But what has that to do with our diamond manufacturing? We already make synthetics.'

Perhaps it's exhaustion, but Loge has to shut his eyes for a moment in despair at his master's ignorance.

'We produce over a million carats of one hundred per cent synthetic diamonds per annum, but the Chinese are ahead of us. Last year, they sold more than this to just five Indian buyers. This invention will enable us massively to increase our capacity, at very low additional cost.'

'We can make more diamonds, cheaper? Good. Get it for me.'

'Sir?'

'Now. Delay is not acceptable. You will receive any support you need. I must have this, Loge. Liaise with my office only.'

'I understand, sir.'

Now he must arrange flights and excuses. He removes his glasses to clean them, while thinking. *How do I, at age seventy-one, come to be working for a despot with no interest in humanity, small or large?* He had been brought up by his grandparents to respect the Soviet culture, and to believe in the triumph of labour over capitalism. Yet his boss is an aggressive capitalist, and he the helpless worker. His wife demands wealth and the respect of a high position in the State, yet modern Russia holds no regard for the dignity of pure science. *It's all about money. I am trapped, and must go to England.*

He feels sure the professor's private email address is not monitored by the university. As he himself uses a secure network, their communication should be free from prying eyes.

Re our conversation, Johns, masterful play. My colleagues wish to discuss your huge potential. They have the resources you need to fulfil your aims. I will let you know when I arrive in Bristol. Check.

Abstract enough, but he feels sure Johns will understand.

A succession of other emails go to Bovar's office to activate travel plans and ensure the resources he might need. *A new game is in play and I will play it face to face with my friend,* Loge thinks. *Let us hope the rendezvous is satisfactory. Valerie will have to wait for her new dress.*

The dawn of a new day in Bristol is of no comfort to Johns. First, it's the throbbing of his temples, then the sour and granular bitterness in his throat, followed by the blunt stabbing headache before – finally – the dazzling light of recognition of what actually happened last night.

The glow of success from achievement in the labs still warms him, but the horror of his failed pass at Polly is, like a cold hand grabbing his entrails. Only then does he acknowledge the terror lurking beneath. Loge knows. How? It doesn't matter. He knows, and the university doesn't.

Johns had ensured backups of the programme were local to the lab, with full duplicates at home. The university servers received only token data. A spoof by him, of course, but of no consequence while he's alive. If he had an accident they would have real cause for concern. That much is good this morning: he is alive.

Two things of which he's certain. One, now that Domino is proven, he must activate the malware.

Two, he must call his boss at the university and alert him to possible industrial espionage.

Surely not? He groans as he rolls out of bed, and pads directly to his laptop. He keeps recordings of all calls, and plays back the conversation with Loge, barely recognizing his own slurred voice. *Embarrassing.* It confirms what he fears. His pulse throbs harder, worsening his headache. *Coffee, I need coffee.* But, out of long habit and fresh fear, he looks first at his emails.

A message from Loge. He reads it ... this is not about chess. He reads it again, trying to put his hangover aside, so he can calibrate the full implications. *Loge is coming to talk about Domino. Who are these mysterious colleagues? Is this genuine?* He feels sure of it. Dismally so.

Johns postpones the call to his principal, and starts calculating the manoeuvres necessary to extricate himself.

Unexpected, but not entirely unwelcome.

Regardless of all claims, I am father and mother to Domino. I own it.

15

THE GUEST

As Saul nudges the BMW expertly past the shutters of the open garage, he feels the deep rumble of the exhaust reverberate from the solid walls around him. He smells the acrid tang of oil and petrol.

With the motorbike duly installed for its service, Saul climbs into the Range Rover beside his brother.

'You're early, bro,' says Albie.

'What does that make you?'

'Hey, Friday afternoon, beautiful weather, cricket on the radio, comfortable car. What's not to like?'

They set off to the pleasant burble of the test match commentary. Saul is silent, until they break the confines of the town, and spill out into the open country. In a private world of pain, until he says, 'What a bunch of monkeys.'

'Etique? That's a surprise, they seemed genuine. Nice woman.'

'The stones are fakes. I was set up by the wife so she could get at her husband.'

Albie gives his brother an old-fashioned look.

'I should have known it was too good to be true,' continues Saul.

'Don't beat yourself up. You're on holiday. The sun's shining and all's well in the world. Just breathe in that good, Wiltshire country air.' The rich odour of manure floods through the open car windows, and the broad smile on Albie's features tells of a farmer at peace with the world.

'Give me the mean streets of the city and the clang of dustbins any day. I really thought I'd got lucky. This one had jackpot written all over it.'

'You never know your luck until you tread in it. Changing the subject, I'm abroad next week for a few days, to look at a farm in Georgia. Zee can feel isolated at the farm and may get anxious, so it'll be good for her to have your company; are you able to hang around?'

'Of course.'

'And we've got the lovely Polly coming to stay. That'll take your mind off things.'

Saul goes for a nap after lunch, exhausted by the heightened emotion of the morning's meetings and flooded with humiliation from Etique. *I, of all people, was so naive on that first meeting. My will to believe in easy money allowed Jeff to sell it to me completely. It was only my training that forced me to do the research which I should have done before ...*

He eventually drops off to sleep, and wakes around four, with fierce sunlight shining directly through the open bedroom window. He can hear the distant sound of cricket commentary on the radio, women's laughter and the baritone of his brother's voice. Looking out, he sees afternoon tea laid out under a garden parasol, the figures with their backs to him, sitting in deckchairs and wearing hats. He grabs a black baseball cap and joins them.

Later, he'd say it was love at first sight.

Albie's ear is bent to the radio in rapt concentration, so Xenia makes the introduction. Polly glances up from beneath the brim of a broad straw hat, fixing Saul with cool sapphire-blue eyes beneath a wisp of gold-blonde hair. The paleness of her skin, the fineness of her bone structure and the slenderness of her arms suggest a dancer rather than a scientist. Both she and Xenia are wearing summer dresses, emphasizing their different complexions. Saul is catapulted back in time to his university days and endless summers. Time stops right there.

'Here.' Xenia passes him a searing-hot mug of tea, which he immediately spills in surprise. 'Would you like some cake, Saul, or shall I just throw it straight onto the grass?'

He's normally quick on the riposte, but not now. He can't find any words, so keeps his mouth shut, smiles, and says to himself, *Get a grip*.

Xenia later tells him that he was frowning.

As he drops into the remaining deckchair, Albie flings himself back with, 'I don't believe it,' as another wicket falls.

'I apologize for the men of the house,' says Xenia, 'They're not normally like this.' The two friends laugh conspiratorially. 'Let's go for a walk.'

Saul watches them stroll away, arm-in-arm.

'So what do you think?' asks Albie.

'Sounds like a bloodbath.'

'Not the cricket, you fool. Polly.'

'Seems pleasant.'

'Ha! I saw you. Dumbstruck.'

'He's what we call in Estonia *krisini lamout* says Polly and, seeing a question mark over Xenia's face, offers a translation: 'A hunk'.

Xenia laughs. 'Saul's a lovely man, but still hurting after a nasty divorce. His ex-wife behaved very badly, and has done all she can to turn his friends against him. He's been working too hard and needs a break; that's why he's here. You've been in Bristol so long, Polly. Don't you miss Estonia?'

'Estonia is my home, and always will be. But there are very few places in the world where I can be part of such ground-breaking scientific research. Bristol is my professional base. It may change, but for now – as I say – we're doing remarkable work with Professor Johns.'

'The lech?'

'This is his only weakness, I think. Ha, we took him for a drink to celebrate last night, and he got wrecked. He doesn't usually touch alcohol.'

'Have I missed your birthday or something?'

'No, no. Between us, we made a huge step forwards in the lab. Giant. Very exciting, but very secret.'

The women return just as the cricket pauses for tea, and Xenia says, 'Silence might be better than two old fogeys chuntering away ... on the radio, I mean,' she adds with a wry smile.

Albie mutes the sound and asks, 'Polly, what are you up to now? Have you saved the world yet?'

'Working on it. We're into diamond surfaces.'

Her voice sounds like a bell to Saul, and seems to echo in a part of him he'd forgotten. He only just manages to get words out. 'Leading-edge,' he says.

'You know about CVD?' enquires Polly.

'I've read reports on how it might be used. Is it really as versatile as they claim?'

'It depends on who you ask, but yes, we've achieved extraordinary adhesion and conductivity, with unique thermal, mechanical, electrical and optical behaviours.' Seeing Albie's raised eyebrows, she laughs. 'You did ask! We believe nano-surfaces could transform many materials.'

'Including a diamond itself?' asks Saul.

'It's a given: carbon on carbon. Unsurprisingly, we use similar equipment and processes to those labs synthesizing diamonds.'

At these words, Saul feels wretched. He forces himself to smile. 'So synthetic stones already exist?'

'Oh, sure. The first patent for them was in 1955. There are even small-scale factories specializing in them. We haven't bothered to surface a diamond for that reason. You're interested, Saul?'

As she says his name, he feels a wave of pleasure flood through his being. He has to consciously breathe deeply to gain self-control, and not grin like an idiot. He senses Albie's eyes on him.

'I've just been learning about the industry.'

'Hmm.' Polly smiles at him.

Saul feels a dangerous rush of excitement.

'Our research is going very well, and the head of our investigation is a genius. Sadly, like most geniuses, he's flawed. I'll put it this way: we don't let him turn the lights down when doing the crystallography. Otherwise, he's fine.'

'I'd like to learn more about your work—'

'We have all weekend, Saul,' interrupts Xenia, a small smile playing on her lips. 'More tea?'

16

COUNTRY WALK

SAUL SLEEPS DEEPLY and well for the first time in many months. His nights have been tormented with unease, since separating from his ex-wife. He's been to a counsellor, but it was no better than a chat over a quiet beer with a good friend. Perhaps several beers, but never enough to be a problem. He gave that up when he realized his waistline was expanding, so took up a furious exercise regime, which typically consumed the first hour of his day. That too is suspended now that he's at the farmhouse.

He wakes to the smell of bacon, and reasons Xenia and Polly must have already left for their forensic examination of the fashion industry's latest offerings in the capital. Albie, therefore, is in the kitchen preparing a fried breakfast, and looking forward to a day out and about, or sitting in front of the cricket. And so it is. They tour the farm in the morning, then Saul's bike must be collected, so they make a trip into town where they adjourn to a local hostelry for a ploughman's lunch. Both eschew alcohol. Back home they watch the English cricket team rally in a heroic batting display, and duly celebrate with a couple of bottles of ale. It's then that Albie remembers that he has to make the evening meal, and corrals his younger brother as sous-chef.

'You must get Xenia to show you her latest creations. They're extraordinary,' says Albie, as he prepares the marinade. Wonderful smells of ginger, fresh coriander and garlic waft across the kitchen. Saul is impressed by his brother's competence as a cook; the only dish he can make reliably is an omelette.

'What's she working on?'

'You'll have to get her to explain; something about crystallography and fractals. It sounds techie, but the results are wonderfully colourful and rich. She has a show booked in London in November.

Saul considers the picture of proud contentment that is his brother. A beautiful farm, a lovely and talented wife; he has every reason to be happy.

'I know what you're thinking – "he's got it easy" – and you're right. It'll happen for you, Saul, I know it. Xenia wants kids – so do I – but it doesn't seem to be in the stars at the moment. Time will tell.'

Behind Albie's matter-of-fact delivery, Saul knows his brother keenly wants a family. The early loss of their parents had been an earthquake for them both. For Albie, grief seems to be a continuous repayment of a debt, rather than a phase of life he has to traverse. Saul, on the other hand, suffered acutely and then clinically reviewed every aspect of his life, including his marriage. This revealed his wife's infidelity. He had walked away, knowing the relationship was radically and irrevocably damaged. That was a year ago, almost to the day. It feels good to be here with Albie today but it also makes the loss more apparent.

He smiles at his older brother. 'Zee's a wonderful person. She adores you.'

Albie smiles broadly and seems to grow in stature. 'I know. I'm a lucky boy.'

Saul has seen the poignant sadness in Xenia's eyes when children are mentioned, but suspects it's because so many friends and neighbours are already blessed with families. He's been to their drinks parties, and seen how much they prize having a talented and interesting mixed-race artist in the community. They like Zee just as she is.

Xenia and Polly arrive back, energized by the trip. They go upstairs, declaring they need to 'wash away the grime of the city' and appear shortly after, immaculate.

'How do you do it?' asks Albie. 'You look like a pair of supermodels,' at which Xenia blushes.

Albie has banned all talk of work or money or politics until Sunday lunchtime, and the laughter and conversation flow freely over supper, lubricated by a generous helping of good wine. By the time they retire for the night, it's after one.

Saul is brushing his teeth when Polly walks in, wearing a T-shirt, loose pyjama trousers and bare feet. Her pale skin and short blonde hair shine in the brightness of the white-tiled room.

'Oh, sorry, Saul.' She smiles softly before retreating, and closing the door.

He pauses, looks at himself in the mirror and sees that, thankfully, he doesn't look too dishevelled. Instinctively, he smooths his hair, then washes his face for a second time. As he returns to his bedroom, there's no one in the corridor, but he hears Polly go back for her own ablutions, then leave once more. His door opens.

'This isn't the bathroom, is it?' she whispers.

Saul laughs. 'No. Have you forgotten something?'

'Yes.' She closes the door softly behind her and walks on tiptoe towards him. Saul feels the blood pounding in his ears and his skin come alive. Polly stands very close to him so he can both hear and feel her breath. She exudes the smell of wild flowers and a bodily warmth. No words are needed.

. . .

There is silence in the house when Saul comes down to make coffee in the morning. He finds a note in Xenia's bold and artistic hand, 'Gone to church.' Their hosts have got up long before and prepared lunch, so Saul and Polly enjoy a discreet breakfast together, before retreating in different directions, to bathe and dress for the day.

A clattering in the kitchen, followed by Ella Fitzgerald singing *Paper Moon* at full volume, signals the churchgoers are back. Saul finds Xenia and Polly in a conspiratorial huddle by the oven.

'Good afternoon, you.' says Xenia, 'Don't you love the music that Polly brought us? Albie's upstairs, that's why he turned it up.' Saul leaves the kitchen to find his brother.

Albie is humming along to Ella as he packs his bags for the trip, 'Good night, bro?'

'Great. Good church? I thought you were just Christmas and Easter.'

'With harvest coming up, we need all the help we can get. Err, you slept in this morning?'

Saul thinks he knows what's coming next, but Albie just grins to himself and returns to his humming.

It doesn't end there, of course. Throughout lunch there are double-entendres and looks between Albie and Xenia whenever Polly or Saul speak to one another.

'I read that a mine sank another British ship off

the coast of Cornwall. Do you know anything about that, Saul?' asks Albie, knowing full well what his brother's been working on.

'Unfortunately, yes. There's a coherent pattern of limpet mine attacks on navies worldwide, both in and out of their home waters. All fingers point to a co-ordinated campaign targeting vessels of wealthy countries.'

'That's an act of war, isn't it?' asks Xenia.

'It depends who you ask. It looks like a major superpower is behind this, so countries will inevitably be slow to point a finger.'

'But you know who it is?'

Saul is silent.

'And ...?'

He shrugs.

Noting Saul's discomfort, Polly speaks up. 'I am Estonian by birth. I detest everything Russia stands for, but I don't think this can originate from them. There is far too much Russian wealth in Britain for them to want to attack this country in any way.'

'Saul?' asks Xenia.

'The Office of National Statistics values Russian assets in the UK at about twenty-five billion pounds, but that's misleading. Most Russian money flows here indirectly, via Britain's offshore satellites, like the British Virgin Islands. Nobody knows for certain how much is held in these British protectorates. One credible estimate is about six hundred billion. Even when it gets here, the assets are held in companies with anonymous directors.'

'There's no proof that cash in offshore companies is dirty,' adds Polly. 'It's done within the law.' She looks at Saul for confirmation, and he nods, but not without disquiet. He knows exactly how easy it is for villains to launder criminal proceeds through property purchases, gambling, shell companies and so on. All of it 'within the law.'

Albie changes the subject swiftly, using his impersonation of a well-known British ex-prime minister with a penchant for mistruths. Within minutes he has his audience sobbing with laughter, and the momentary tension is dispelled.

He segues into an anecdote. 'I travelled round South Africa when I was seventeen. Early one Sunday morning I found myself alone in the central district of Jo'burg near a big department store. This rough-looking black African dude in raggedy clothes comes up to me and says, "Do you want to buy a diamond?" Naturally, I say yes. So, he brings this stone out, walks up to a huge plate-glass window, and scrapes a foot-long scar across it. I suddenly get frightened because here was this skinny – yeah, thanks Saul – skinny kid from England, with all the money he owned in his pocket. I remember the look in the guy's eyes to this day. A look of true desperation.'

'Did you buy the rock?' asks Polly.

'No. I wanted to give him money, but couldn't do it without showing him I was, relatively speaking, loaded. He was a grown man, probably with a family that he never got to see. I was a snotty-nosed, foreign kid. I felt bad.'

'Also, you thought it was a fake,' says Xenia.

Albie laughs. 'I guess I did. I'll never know.'

'You're smart, Albie, it's very easy to fool someone when they want to believe,' says Polly.

Saul feels stung by the remark, but dismisses it as him being oversensitive after the farrago with Etique.

Again, Albie steps in, 'OK, time for a walk. I want to show Polly the new boar.'

'My husband knows how to give a guest a good time!' says Xenia, and they head out beneath the blue sky of another perfect summer afternoon, to see the pigs.

After Albie has shown off the new piglets in the sty with their mother, he uses Saul to demonstrate the finer points of persuading a prize boar to move from one churned field to another. This requires his brother to carry a bucket of nuts, with the pig in hot pursuit, again reducing them all – other than Saul – to helpless laughter. Afterward, Xenia and Polly hang back from the boys, who walk on ahead.

'Is something up, Pol?'

'Just seeing those cute piglets with their mother.'

'Yes, and ...?'

'I might be pregnant.'

'Really! Actually, I did see the positive test in the bathroom bin when I emptied it.'

'It's the third time I've done the test. It's not straightforward.'

'Oh, I'm sorry, Polly.'

'I'm seeing a doctor tomorrow.'

'Could you be a mum and do your work?'

Silence.

'You'll let me know straight away? Will you WhatsApp me?' asks Xenia, looking directly into her eyes.

'I'll use Telegram. It's more confidential.'

'OK, I'll download it later. Albie's going abroad tomorrow so if you want to talk, I'm all yours. You know you can always come here if you need help. Saul can go back up to town anytime. Will you promise me you'll call as soon as you know?'

'Sure. Thanks.'

Xenia and Polly walk on in silence, arm in arm.

17

THE ACCOUNTANT

LOGE CATCHES a regular flight to the UK, requiring a connection in Amsterdam. A driver meets him at the London Heathrow arrivals area with a sign for 'Princorps'. In the terminal car park, he escorts Loge to a large black MPV with tinted windows. Drawing back the side door, he reveals a compact, carpeted mobile office with four comfortable chairs in dark velour, clustered around a small, grey table. The Accountant sits waiting. A small, dark man in a charcoal grey suit. His skin looks like it hasn't seen sun or air for a decade, and his face is badly pockmarked. Despite the top note of an expensive fabric cleaner, Loge detects a distant whiff of mothballs and cologne.

Loge accepts his unsmiling host's cool and slightly damp hand in greeting.

'Welcome to the UK, sir. Your flight was good?'

'I slept. Old men need sleep.'

'In that case, I won't waste your time.' The Accountant tells the driver to depart. 'We'll travel to your hotel this evening. Tomorrow morning we'll attend the Materials Research facility at SouthWest University. Professor Johns is awaiting your visit, I understand?'

'Correct.'

'We'll be joined there by our security detail with additional transport. They will ensure that all necessary assets are transferred. I have the offer ready, together with documentation for your receipt. I need you to countersign.'

'Do you have everything prepared for our final destination?'

The Accountant draws some aerial pictures and a map out of a side pocket, and opens it to show Loge the location and surrounding terrain. A lone cottage sits at the top end of a private valley, down which a small stream has cut a gulley to the shoreline about a mile distant. The watercourse is almost covered in thick scrub for the first half of its journey, then in the open as it nears the shore. The photos are remarkably distinct, and show the cottage with a large outbuilding set at right angles to it. There's no other habitation nearby.

The coastline at the far end of the valley is flecked with white surf and a line of black rocks taper out to sea from a tiny, slate-grey beach. A path, visible on both the map and images, hugs the edge of the coast and crosses the stream at ninety degrees.

'The cottage has been swept for monitoring devices and is clean, apart from our own. We've been careful to leave no trace of our visit. The only drawback is there's no mobile signal, which compromises our system. As you see, the location is very remote. Amusingly, there's a large military defence facility quite close by – about three miles – but not near enough for any concern. We can enter and leave the site unobserved.'

Loge does not find it at all amusing, but lets it go. It has been cleared by security and that is enough.

18

CAPTIVE

THE HOTEL IS what Loge has come to expect from his many years of business travel. A large, uncomfortable bed, with four even more uncomfortable pillows, a TV, a bathroom. Functional, bland and airless.

He's confident that his internet activity cannot be tracked by the UK's GCHQ. He always observes strict security protocols but, equally, he knows every communication to and from his laptop will be logged at home in Russia. He has some decoy tactics to circumvent this, but this morning he makes no changes, as he checks on the various strings of R&D underway at Bovar Industries. It's his habit to deal with emails at the beginning of the day, while his mind is at its sharpest. Breakfast follows.

The appointment at the labs is for nine. Every minute that passes is a cause for concern, lest Johns let his contractual obligation to the university overrule his personal interests. Loge calculates this is not greater than a thirty-three per cent. likelihood.

Leaving the hotel main entrance, he blinks in the strong sunshine of the August morning. Two identical black MPVs draw up, and the side door of the front vehicle slides open immediately. Inside is the sombre face of the Accountant, together with a sharp-suited, hatchet-faced young man, who seems to be expecting trouble, or at least the opportunity to create it. Loge knows the type and, in that moment – irrationally, he thinks – he fears for his son, Victor.

'Good morning, sir,' begins the Accountant. 'Journey time is twenty-five minutes. There are three further security personnel in the car behind, and a further van at the rendezvous. They will transport any and all necessary assets to the safe house, and we will accompany them. I have the money with me and ask you to examine it before we make the offer. Are you certain they'll accept?'

'Nothing is certain.'

'Just so. We have three options, all of which require our target to travel with us to the safe house. It's essential we achieve repatriation and full ownership of the intellectual property.'

'I understand.' Loge loathes this little man's cold self-importance. He makes nothing, and understands less.

'Option one is for Professor Johns to accept a substantial cash allowance in full payment.'

'That's not going to happen.'

The Accountant nods, primly. 'The second is for both this cash inducement, and up to five million pounds sterling. The amount you propose is at your discretion, and I suggest starting at one million.'

Loge nods. He does not like to negotiate. The mention of such riches causes a lurch in the pit of his stomach. He thinks of Valerie's response to such an offer, and his own relative poverty, after a lifetime of faithful work.

The Accountant pauses, blatantly struggling to read Loge's impassive features. 'Finally, a situation we would like to avoid: the threat of death. Obviously, we do not expect you to suggest this ... ah ... directly.'

Now it's Loge's turn to examine his handler. Where is the compassion in this creature, whose air he is forced to share? The vehicle glides smoothly on towards the lab. He feels sick that he's unwittingly imperilled Johns. *Such one-pointed dedication. He deserves protection.*

'I will go in with just two men and require you to wait. We'll let you know if there is any difficulty in the negotiation,' says Loge.

'But—' complains the Accountant, only to be silenced by Loge's broad raised hand.

. . .

Johns is already in the lab when Polly arrives, and the signs of his high anxiety are clear to her. Here is a man who masters vast and abstruse mathematical theorems but finds it impossible to relax. Under pressure, his nervous smile is supplemented by a twitch in the top of his right cheek, or an involuntary squint of both eyes. In extreme circumstances the two would fire alternately ... a twitch, a squint, a twitch, a squint. A lousy poker player, thinks Polly, catching her boss winking manically as he turns away to hide his face.

'We have a VIP visit this morning,' Johns snaps. 'I've called administration and given Lucy and Anna the day off. We don't want the lab too full.'

'Who?'

'A new corporate sponsor.'

It was always like this before a big meeting. Johns hates changes to his routine, and Monday mornings are sacrosanct to him. She has long accepted his neuroses, in the light of his extraordinary intellect.

'When do they arrive?'

'Any minute.'

Polly sees Johns is not merely tense, but deeply agitated. Despite his attempts to hide them, she sees a rapid twitch of his mouth and quick clenches of the fingers.

'I'll make tea.'

'No. Yes. Tea would be good.'

As she walks towards the kitchen, she hears the swing doors in the corridor behind her and the heavy steps of three males. She turns to see an elderly gentleman with a briefcase, accompanied by two much younger figures. They knock at Johns' office.

Polly calls over her shoulder, 'He's in the lab. I'll be with you in a moment. Do you want tea?'

'That's not necessary, thank you.'

She pauses, then enters the kitchen, synapses firing. She knows the signs, and focuses her mind with long deep abdominal breaths.

Loge is surprised that Johns is not taller or more imposing. What he finds is a shabby creature, almost furtive, dressed in a tattered tweed sports jacket with thick leather patches on the elbows, an un-ironed, once-white shirt and crumpled dark trousers. Though the professor's face is remarkable for its pallor, his dark eyes shine with a startling animation and fervour. This is someone I can work with, thinks Loge.

'Welcome, welcome,' says Johns, looking directly at his guest, then hesitatingly at the menacing figures behind him. 'I wasn't expecting such a large party.'

'Nor I,' says Loge, trying to reassure his friend with as much warmth and sincerity in his eyes as in his voice.

'Polly's getting tea ...' says Johns, at which she

enters with two mugs, sets them down on a lab desk and turns. As she extends her hand in greeting, Loge is astonished. His mouth goes dry. He knows her. She slips her hand from his grasp after the briefest of shakes and nods formally to the dark-suited young men. They show no interest in their surroundings and acute interest in her.

Johns breaks the silence, saying, 'Let's get started' too loudly; his voice cannons and reverberates from the hard surfaces and pipework around them. He conducts Loge through the facility and, together with Polly, gives a broad overview of the process. Finally, he shows the fruit of their research through the electron microscope.

'Very impressive, Professor. I'm convinced,' says Loge.

'This is a very great breakthrough. I flatter myself, and my team of course,' he says, looking admiringly at Polly, 'that this is of global importance.'

'Indeed it is. Worthy of a Nobel, I think.'

At the mention of such august recognition, Johns seemed transfigured with joy. 'I'm honoured you might consider it worthy.'

Loge raises his hands in modesty. 'It is the jury, not I who must be convinced!' he intones, trying to soften the man before the brutal reality of what is to come. He looks at Polly for any glimmer of recognition from her.

She looks back, unblinking.

Loge gently warms his palms on one another. 'As I've indicated, my employers are prepared to make an investment. Shall we discuss this in your office?'

'No, we can talk here. I'm not a businessman, Loge.'

'I am authorized to make all necessary arrangements to give you, together with whatever equipment you need, the equivalent of five million pounds sterling in any currency you nominate. I have an advance payment in this briefcase. But I know money is of little concern to you.' Loge can see, in fact, the sum clearly means a great deal to Johns. 'So in addition, I personally commit to sponsoring a presentation of your work for international recognition at the highest level.'

The effect is electrifying. There seems to be no doubt whatsoever in Johns, who nods vigorously.

'Yes, yes, of course. The contents of the laboratory belong to the university; they need to be replicated. I also require Polly to accompany me as an assistant. She would be established as my junior partner in this discovery. Is that acceptable?'

If Polly is surprised by this turn of events, she doesn't show it. 'What does this mean, Professor?'

'Do we need to discuss it?'

'You propose we leave the university and work for a single corporate entity?' she says, sounding dazed, but her blue eyes steady, looking directly at him.

'If I may; Polly …?' says Loge, waiting an additional beat. She looks steadily into his eyes. He sees no flicker of recognition or challenge. 'I am old. You have your life ahead of you. If you choose to accompany the professor, I can assure you of fame, wealth and scientific fulfilment.'

Johns seems to have grown in both enthusiasm and confidence. 'We can do this, Polly.'

'What will become of me if I say no?'

'Of course you are free to go,' says Johns, 'but please don't.'

'Lucy and Anna? What will happen with them?'

'I'll give them first-class testimonials,' says Johns. 'They will easily find other employment.'

'OK,' says Polly in a small voice, looking down.

'Excellent, there is no time to waste,' says Loge. 'Professor Johns, these gentlemen will travel with you to your home in Cornwall, where I understand you have already installed serviceable equipment. We will provide whatever else you need and, be assured, your welfare is my highest priority. I need you to make a copy of the programme for me, and I will give you this briefcase. You can then collect your belongings and we will depart.'

Johns gapes, slack-jawed for a moment, then springs into manic action. 'Polly, please come to my office. Gentlemen, we need some time. Shall we meet you downstairs?'

‘No, we wait here. Please do not delay,’ says Loge.

Johns goes straight to the desktop in his office. He double-checks the malware is activated, makes a nominal update to the university servers, then transfers a copy of Domino to a USB stick together with the embedded malware. At the same time, he supervises Polly in the collection of notebooks, while she peppers him with questions. Within minutes they’re on their way back to the lab with hard drives and logbooks. Johns leaves the office without a glance. In that shining moment, all that matters is his glorious future with Polly.

19

WORRIED

THE HOUSE IS empty when Saul wakes. He knew Zee was planning to drop Albie at Heathrow for the red-eye. She would then go on to the gallery in London to discuss her upcoming exhibition.

Saul spends the day writing in his room, descending only to make coffee and then grab some fruit for lunch. It's after four when Xenia returns with a 'Hi' up the stairs, and after six when he comes down to the kitchen to find her cooking supper. She offers him wine and Saul notes a packet of cigarettes and a green plastic lighter conspicuously poking over the edge of a shelf. They weren't there earlier in the day.

'You don't smoke, Zee!'

'I'm worried, Saul. Polly hasn't called.'

'You only saw her yesterday.'

'She had an important meeting today; she

promised ... a work thing.' Xenia hates telling lies, but the doctor's visit had been a confidence between her and Polly. 'She said she'd need to talk it through.'

Saul looks steadily at her, unconvinced.

Xenia gives a mysterious smile. 'You're fond of her, aren't you?'

Saul affects insouciance.

'Don't give me that look. That's exactly what your brother does. Bloody public school education. It doesn't teach you the first thing about anything important, like feelings.' She gives a hollow laugh.

'Busted,' says Saul, raising his arms in mock surrender.

'I've sent her a message on Telegram – we tested it before she left, so I know it works – but nothing.'

'Zee, I'm sure she's fine. If it's important, she'll call.'

Xenia smiles. 'Of course, I'm worrying unnecessarily. It's good to have you here.' There's hesitation in her voice, but Saul can hear she's reassured.

20

THE PRIZE

Bovar leans his gross bulk back into the frame of his desk chair, resting both hands on the huge walnut desk before him. He allows himself a moment to dwell on what he might buy with further wealth from diamonds: a bigger yacht, an extension to the house in Provence, or perhaps a second mistress? *Everything has consequences,* he muses. He levers himself forward, aided by the powerful spring in his seat, and demands his secretary put in a call to Vasiliev and Bychkov. 'Wherever they are and whatever they're doing, and get the group head of diamond fabrication on the line.'

He then sends Loge a one-word email: *Update.*

Bovar pulls up a dashboard on his desktop screen, showing the current production of stones across his four diamond manufacturing plants within Russia. The data includes the market price per carat, manufacturing costs and current sales trends. The phone rings.

'Tymchenko from diamonds here, sir.'

'What is our shortfall in meeting market demand for lab diamonds at our current price per carat?'

'We estimate we need at least twenty times capacity, sir. Might we be able to buy more machines? If so ...'

'Stop, Tymchenko. I've solved this. You'll be hearing from Loge in the near future.'

'Yes, sir.'

The other phone rings. Bovar cuts Tymchenko off.

'Sir, I have Vasiliev and Bychkov on the line.'

'Put them through.'

'I've left a board meeting for this and they're waiting.' It's Vasiliev.

'You will find this highly agreeable,' states Bovar, 'but we seem to be missing Mr Bychkov.'

'Here.'

'Excellent, excellent.' How Bovar enjoys playing cat and mouse with these two. He considers wasting their time further, just for the pleasure of it, but senses it's time to show his hand. 'I have an offer for you.'

'Yes,' comes the reply, almost in unison.

'Diamonds. In return for your help, I'm giving you immediate access to enormous wealth, by enabling you to flood the market with diamonds.

Bovar Industries have already established good production and a proven route to market for laboratory-created stones. Retailers pass these off as mined, ensuring them a handsome margin. We now have a technology breakthrough to increase production ten-fold at nominal cost. There will be a ready market, even at the wholesale price for mined diamonds.

'What's the catch?' asked Bychkov.

'Ha, we creatures of commerce are all the same, Uri! There is no catch. You will only have to make a modest contribution to The State. I'm sure you're already aware of this.'

'Let me get this straight, Bovar.' The staccato tones of Vasiliev indicate high excitement. 'You propose to cede your entire diamond manufacturing arm to us as full payment. Is that correct?'

'You have it in one.'

'What about the diamond mining operations?' says Bychkov.

'I keep them. What I offer you is the future. The profitability in diamond mining is modest, with huge overheads and political battles to fight. And don't get me started on the fucking eco-warriors and do-gooder human-rights-crazies. Instead, manufacturing is predictable, sleek and, with this new technology, extremely profitable.'

'I don't trust new technology,' counters Vasiliev,

who has a shrewd idea of the margin Bovar enjoys from his mines.

'This is a certainty. It works. It is tested and proven. There is no risk.'

A further pause. Bovar understands the men have established a back-channel for communication. He waits, amused, confident.

Vasiliev speaks first. 'OK, it makes sense. We need exclusivity on the intellectual property, free access to the technology creators, all diamond capacity from your current manufacturing, and a licence to operate the entire system without competition from you in manufacturing. Is that acceptable?'

Bovar has anticipated this. He only wants the mines; they're big, highly profitable, politically powerful businesses he understands and likes. 'Agreed.'

'We have a deal, then,' says Bychkov. 'Please send us the agreement.'

'It will be with you at the end of the week. You will start receiving material from tomorrow, including the performance dashboard, so you can monitor your profits. The creators of the system are in the UK, and we'll begin proceedings to transfer them to your care immediately. My head of technology is already with them. Thank you, gentlemen.'

Bovar ends the call. He reaches out a thick hand

to draw two fat dossiers compiled by Kalov. They include detailed descriptions of Vasiliev and Bychkov's illicit activities in the UK and overseas, all operational details on the limpet mine attacks, and the tactics used to sweeten government ministers and media in various countries. There is plenty to read.

He feels confident that the alliance of Vasiliev and Bychkov is a partnership of convenience. *They would love to tear each other apart, given the chance. I look forward to that.*

21

DEPARTURE

THE PICK-UP TEAM transport Johns and Polly, in separate vehicles, to collect clothes and belongings from their respective homes. Polly feels the eyes of her sentinel closely on her as they enter the flat. Her hackles rise, and she has to fight to quell her sense of outrage when the smartly dressed goon tells her, 'Ten minutes.'

'What's your name?' she asks.

He hesitates. 'Ivan.'

She appraises him, determined to take control. *He's clean, at least. Doesn't look intelligent, but is physically assured. Probably ex-military; he has that way with him. But not trained in Europe: too stiff and mannered. Wary rather than watchful, so perhaps he's nervous. No wedding ring and he looks single – probably desperate for a girlfriend.* 'Well, Ivan, I suggest you tell your friends I'll be ready when I'm ready. This is all unplanned.' She smiles at him. 'Please, make yourself comfortable.'

'We cannot stay.'

'I'm not thinking of staying, I just need time.' With this, Polly turns smartly on her heel, strides into her bedroom and closes the door.

He grunts, as though it's of no interest, but she hears him calling the driver with anxiety in his voice. She changes from work clothes into a white T-shirt, black leather trousers and white pumps. Half an hour later, they emerge to find the MPV missing from the parking slot.

'He's avoiding detection because you were so long,' explains Ivan, two steps behind her with three large bags, just as the car appears at the end of the street.

'What the fuck?' demands the driver.

Ivan shrugs. 'The luggage,' he says, as he hurriedly stows Polly's bags, then runs to jump in the front next to the driver. Polly waits outside with her black backpack.

'What now?' Ivan asks.

She looks at him, head on one side, plainly waiting for him to open the side door.

Ivan clambers back out, slides it open and waves her in. Johns is already in the MPV cabin, blinking in speechless surprise. Polly smiles, pleased to see the effect her change of clothes has made.

The driver glares at Ivan, 'It'll be three and a half hours,' he snaps.

Again, Ivan shrugs.

Ninety minutes later, they turn off the motorway and pass along roads of diminishing size. They dive and climb their way through a series of steeply wooded valleys. As the people carrier crests a hill, Johns gives a childlike gasp of excitement, as he sees the blue of the sea through the tinted window. He tries to open it.

'Can I have some air in here?' he asks the driver, who unlocks it. Sweet country air floods the cabin. He nods, in a reverie. 'We're very close now,' he says.

They slow to well below regulation speed as they pass a long stretch of steel fencing and barbed wire surrounding the military base. Within are huge satellite dishes, radar domes like giant golf balls and low-slung buildings. Polly asks Johns about the facility, but he shrugs in disinterest. She's not fooled by the faded red-and-white signs warning 'Danger, Keep Out', nor the fact the fence and wire are just two or three metres high. Judging from the array, she understands this is a highly active site for signals intelligence. *Spying*.

Shortly after, they turn onto an unsigned track lined with gorse. They follow it down about half a mile, over increasingly rough ground, to an isolated thatched cottage. Polly is pleasantly surprised by the aspect of the house. Though the windows are set low, it's more substantial than she'd anticipated, with moulded thatch arches over the windows on the upper floor. It holds a dominant position at the apex of a long shallow gorge that runs down to the sea about a mile distant. A small stream tumbles audibly near the house. She sees it sparkle in the sunlight, as it emerges from the brush lower down, and finally spills into a tiny narrow outlet. Uplifting. Romantic, even. She then reminds herself who she's with and why she's there.

The other MPV pulls up alongside them, on the patchwork of dried mud and white-grey granite gravel that serves as turning circle. A commanding figure, with large brown eyes and improbably long eyelashes steps out from the front seat. He's tall and upright, and radiates authority; made faintly absurd by the hoodie and pressed jeans that he wears. He's immediately joined by three others, who stand strictly to attention. Their clothing – all variations on the theme established by their leader – ensures any of them might be mistaken for walkers from the coast path. Equally their rigid stance, powerful chests and gaunt faces attest to severe military training. There's a pause while Ivan opens the side door for Polly and Johns, then he and the driver join the honour guard.

The group leader addresses them. 'Welcome home to your home Mr Johns, Ms Smith. I am

Sokolov and appointed as your senior protection officer.' He speaks perfect English with an authority that demands certainties. He smiles and does not blink. *His eyes have seen too much,* Polly thinks. 'Please let me or my team know of anything you require, no matter how small. We have an additional squad stationed nearby and I'm confident we can deal with any situation. Do you have questions?'

'Where will you stay?' asks Johns.

'You're unlikely to see more than one of us at any time, unless you leave the premises. Our orders are to provide safe escort. I'm sure you understand. My men will help you with your bags.'

If Polly's first impression of the house is positive, the second is less so. Johns pushes the door open against a pile of post which has accumulated in the three months since he was last there. Despite the warm weather, the house smells of damp, old paper and clay. The slate floor of the hallway doesn't look as though it's ever seen a mop. Slugs have left faint, silvery trails across the grubby stone flags. Polly recoils at the smell of ancient sour milk and unemptied bins. It brings up bad memories from her first term at uni, when she had the misfortune to share a house with five girls who eschewed housekeeping.

'We need some help with the house,' she declares to Johns, and turns to Ivan bringing up the bags behind them. 'Please ensure we have all necessary items for cleaning.'

She marches to the kitchen and asks Johns where everything is. Within minutes she's compiled a list of supplies, and hands it to the waiting Ivan. 'Immediately, please,' she commands.

Since arriving, Johns has hovered around Polly like an anxious moth. She sees he needs to feel in control, so smiles demurely.

'Let me show you to your room,' he says, and leads the way up the heavily creaking, narrow stairs, lined on either side by white-painted tongue and groove boards, set vertically. The stairwell opens onto a surprisingly sunny landing which, Polly is relieved to register, smells drier than downstairs. 'My room is here,' he waves to the right, 'and yours ...' he opens his palm to the door next to it. 'They both look onto the sea.'

'Thank you, Professor. I need to freshen up.' Backpack over her shoulder, Polly enters her room, shuts the door, and flings her luggage onto the nearer of the two single beds. She walks slowly to the window. It opens with a groan of rusted hinges. Air rushes into the room to fill the vacuum of staleness caused by unkempt bedding, damp wool rugs and ancient floorboards. She's rewarded with the smell of meadows and the sea mixed with the brittle-sweet freshness of the tinder-dry thatch. Ten minutes later,

Polly is downstairs, washed, hair brushed and changed for a run.

'I'm going out.'

'Do you want me to show you —?'

'I'm good,' she says as she wrenches open the door a little too hard. It shudders in its frame as though she's assaulted a frail, old lady. She smiles wryly, and steps out onto the turning circle, noting its slight slope away from the house, before the irregular hedge of shrubs and dusty gorse. The long sweep of the valley stretches out beyond, ending where the stream meets the sea. She sets off with a loose-limbed jog through gaps in the low scrub, to find and follow the path of the water. She can hear one of the guards not far behind, but doesn't turn to see.

As she comes closer to the coastline, the undergrowth disappears, so she picks her way along the cutting of the brook. Reaching the coast path, she walks up the side of the steep escarpment on the west side of the valley. At the crest she finds a dramatic promontory perpendicular to the path, jutting a jagged finger out into the sea. A narrow horizontal ridge of beaten earth and fine gravel stretches to the very tip. It's unworn. A vertiginous three-hundred-foot slope falls away on either side.

Polly hesitates and does a quarter turn to check the guard in her peripheral vision. She feels her breaths shorten with the mixture of adrenaline and fear. She knows she must go straight ahead and walks forward, commanding her purpose to reign. Her legs begin to shake at the halfway point, but she can't stop now. Polly focuses on the peak ahead, inhaling deeply and gritting her teeth. Arriving at the peak, she forces herself to look over the tip into the moil of the ocean below. A sudden rush of nervous energy forces her to her knees. She sits, and feels her arms, legs and neck fizzing with the conflict between her fears and her will. Far below, the ever-surging sea is like a massive beast that wants to draw her into its unknown depths. She twists a hundred and eighty degrees and looks back towards the mainland. The guard has remained on the coast path, watching intently. The cottage is out of sight from here, but below and at the foot of the cliffs, the little stream gushes out onto slate-grey pebbles washed black by its waters. Further out to sea, skinny lines of dark rock stretch out from the coastline like bony fingers, their knuckles protruding through the rise and fall of the briny waves.

Further to the west, and not more than two or three miles, she can clearly see the dishes and golf balls marking the military base.

Just then, a jet fighter bursts over the top of the hill, breaking the silence with a shattering roar. Polly turns back to the sea and lets out a long deep scream at the top of her lungs, inaudible beneath the violent howl of the engines. Momentarily dizzy, one part of her feels alarmed, another exhilarated. Deep emotional currents surge within her as she fights to regain self-possession. She trembles, as she comprehends the danger of her position, and slumps forward, holding her head in her hands. *It's all out of control.*

As she raises her head once more, all she can really sense is the brilliant light of the sun contrasting with the dark shadows of the cliff faces, and the jagged slabs of rock on these time-tested cliffs. She feels suspended between nature and something unnatural, as though the sea itself is alive. As Polly stands, to walk back along the ridge, she feels as though part of her has remained, falling, extinguished, collapsing into a pit of endless anguish and claimed as a lost soul.

The first full day of Johns' and Polly's isolation at the cottage breaks with a clear, blue sky and the rich birdsong of a dawn chorus in the valley. Johns wakes to the unfamiliar noise of Polly's hairdryer in the room next door. Over breakfast, he outlines the necessary steps to prepare his home laboratory for meaningful work. Although the equipment in the outbuilding was fully commissioned on installation, they need to calibrate the settings with the university lab. It's just a matter of retrieving the settings from one of the hard drives and updating the system.

His shopping list for Loge includes multiple

high-performance materials, together with hydrocarbon, and other rare gases; the first delivery arrives later that day via the security team. Johns is gratified to see his and Polly's work being treated with proper respect by their new partners, but now feels deeply uneasy about letting the university down. There had been a short talk with Loge about smoothing the way, with a substantial endowment to the college, but Johns now realizes this is a fantasy. *Life is short,* he reflects.

The following day, Johns is up earlier. He makes himself coffee and looks out of the kitchen window at the gently rolling ocean waves, sparkling in the distance, against the V of the descending, green valley. *Perfect. I can do my work, I have Polly by my side and the promise of all the wealth and professional resources I'll ever need. Even Polly seems happy to be here.*

She is still out on her morning run and had told him, with a mischievous smile, that she aimed to lose the 'extremely creepy' guard, who'd been posted to keep her under observation.

For himself, Johns hopes she'll wear the same outfit as yesterday. His mouth goes dry at the thought, and he finishes his coffee.

He walks over towards the outbuilding, and congratulates himself on his foresight in ensuring a three-phase energy supply from a huge diesel generator. He's not a practical man, but in attention to his work, he is meticulous. He checks the fuel and starts the motor. The soundproof box dampens the cacophony, but the stench of diesel ... *the combustion engine is a problem that needs a solution*, he thinks, *but we need plenty of electricity for this venture.* Entering the makeshift lab, he switches on the power-conditioning unit. Lights – entirely unnecessary in the brilliance of a summer's day – flicker to life. The reassuring hum of equipment fills the air. It's cool in the room, but it will soon warm from both the heat of the electronics and the sun beating on the three skylight windows.

We'll need air conditioning, but this can be added to the list for Loge.

The heating and light in the cottage remain on gas. There's no telephone and the mobile signal is non-existent. He's always enjoyed being off-grid and inaccessible, *and now it's proving valuable*, he thinks to himself. *Anyway, it's a delight in summer to go for a short stroll up the side of the valley to make a call. A real delight, and a small price to pay for peace.* He winces at the throbbing racket from the generator outside, but soothes himself with the knowledge of the power it brings.

22

B & B

Everywhere in the far west of the UK is fully booked for the summer, with hundreds of thousands of holidaymakers congesting the roads, beaches, ice-cream sellers and doctors' surgeries. On a sunny day in August, almost everyone is either on the beach or trying to get there. A steady crawl of one-way traffic approaching the coastal town of Bude, belches incongruous fumes. The tiny high street is festooned by fluorescent children's buckets, spades and floats; the cars creep past little cafes and bakeries all proclaiming 'the best pasty in Cornwall'.

Nowhere in the centre of this bustling metropolis, blessed with neither rail connections nor hospital, is there somewhere for Loge to stay. Not among the ancient granite cottages, nestled in the shade of steep-sided wooded valleys, in the vicinity of Johns' cottage, nor in the featureless housing on the yawning iron-flat hilltop favoured by the military base. The only available accommodation is in a pale and pleasant suburb, on a narrow street studded with cream and pastel-coloured villas of varying architectural styles. The Accountant apologizes for the inconvenience of the location, and arranges a hire car for his esteemed guest.

In the late evening sunlight, Loge inspects the tiny sky-blue Nissan. He looks up from the car and examines the plain white cement render exterior of his bed and breakfast. This is all that's left at short notice, and that's fine by him. *I'm in Britain, the weather is fine and the transfer of Johns has been made without unpleasantness.* The security detail has strict instructions to observe and shield, but not to interfere. *They seem to be obedient. The Accountant has gone back to London; good riddance to him.*

Loge likes simplicity, and his accommodation is definitely simple. They have broadband, but his laptop informs him the transmission of Domino will take a further eight hours. He decides to go for a short walk to admire the evening sky.

When he returns to his room, he pauses the upload and calls Bovar on his personal number. It's late in Moscow. Loge allows himself a small, grim smile at the likely inconvenience to his employer.

'Bovar.'

'Sir, I'm transferring the programme to you now.

Due to file size and bandwidth issues, it will take some hours.'

'Does it work?'

'The potential is astonishing.'

'Tell me, Loge. Don't be vague.'

'I see immediate applications for us in three areas. One, is military. We need immediate R&D to test the surfacing material in different applications, specifically for body armour and weapons hardening, but it's useful for so much more. Two, is in diamond manufacturing: we can immediately move – at the flick of a switch – to making large, pure diamonds in our CVD units. These will be indistinguishable from natural stones with no telltale chemical elements that a scanner might detect. We'll use the same formula in the mass production of small stones in our other units, but this will take longer to implement. Ultimately, it will greatly increase our productivity of diamonds with nominal investment. Finally, there are general commercial uses, too many to number.'

'How much is all this going to cost me?'

'Whatever you choose. You've already paid the capital. The return on investment will be colossal.'

'Colossal.' Bovar rolls the word around his mouth as though tasting an exquisite sweetmeat. Loge can hear his master's saliva, and is disgusted.

'When do I get this?'

'By morning your time, sir. I paused the transfer to ring you.'

'Then you'd better get off the line, hadn't you?' The call ends abruptly.

Loge takes a moment to consider Bovar's response, and concludes his employer is more than excited by his new acquisition.

He turns his mind to the paradox of Polly. *Before Victor went to the military academy. In St Petersburg. Was it eight, or nine years ago? She came to our home. Now she is here, in Britain, working with a prominent scientist. Extraordinary.*

Loge wakes early in anticipation of a further encounter with his boss. He is bathed, dressed and settled at his own laptop with a cup of English breakfast tea by 6 a.m.

At 8.30 Moscow time, two hours ahead of the UK, Bovar is grinding his teeth, seated at his desk. He's impatient to activate Domino. He calls his secretary to get Loge on the line.

A visibly trembling *apparatchik* from IT installs the programme, 'I must run a virus check.'

'There is no need. Leave.'

The phone rings.

'I have Domino on my machine. Now what?' Bovar demands of Loge.

'Please open it in the normal way, sir.'

On opening the programme, Bovar's screen is filled with a form. 'What's the meaning of this?'

Why is it, no matter how many times I tell them, my underlings insist on springing surprises that require me to respond immediately? Don't they understand what pressure I'm under? Don't they see that I employ them to relieve my pressure? My time is valuable; no, sacred. How dare they impinge on my goodwill? Again, and again, my staff force me to endure a cycle of patiently waiting for an explanation, then more patience, then more explanations. I'm a reasonable man; I just doesn't want to be made to think.

'The programme requires you take ownership, sir,' says Loge. 'It requires metadata in a digital vault. This identifies you as the beneficiary of any and all licences granted on the formula in this specific copy.'

I'm sick of these zauchka ... these nerds, with their permissions and passwords and jargon, thinks Bovar. *Is Loge trying to put me down?*

'I don't need this, I own it already,' he explodes, grinding his teeth with frustration. He does not, of course, deny the importance of identifying himself as the owner. *No one will usurp my right to the wealth that will flow from this.* He breathes deeply, as his doctor has advised him. 'Talk me through it.'

'The programme generates a unique identifier in the blockchain, which ensures all royalty payments go to your account.'

'Is it safe?' asks Bovar, who has heard dimly of a blockchain.

'It's an irreversible digital contract. It is one hundred per cent secure.'

Bovar knows better than most about how money flows. In his case, income pours from multiple sources into a single clearing account, a holding bank, which automatically distributes it to his personal accounts around the world.

'Are you using your laptop for both this call and for registration?' asks Loge.

'Yes. So, my name, company, clearing account details, and password for the account ... this is definitely secure?'

'Entirely. It's exclusive to you.'

Bovar completes the ledger and, with a stab of his thick index finger, hits the return key with relish. A further box comes up with 'Step Two – Fingerprint.'

'It's asking me for a fingerprint.' He deliberately dials a note of threat into his voice.

'You can do this later. It is simply added security. Click on the box and it will clear.'

'It's done. I am now the absolute owner, correct?'

'Yes, sir. Any subsidiary owners must complete the same process. Of course, once they do so, they will receive income from their distinct operation to their individual accounts.'

'OK, Loge, you can go now. I've authorised the military R&D, and I expect results soon. I also want you to talk with Tymchenko in diamonds about implementing Domino immediately. Is that clear?'

'Yes, sir.' The line goes dead.

Silently, and unknown to either Bovar or Loge, the malware immediately opens secret doors. It easily bypasses local virus detection and interrogates the host laptop for passwords and financial details. Online computer conversations with Bovar's personal accounts commence. A port is opened for Johns to take control, whenever he wants.

The threshold that allows the safe testing of Domino is not yet passed, but the way is being prepared. As soon as the trigger point is exceeded, Domino will commence buying doomed stocks and bad currency positions. The malware will exploit credit held in any account related to the owner, and use it as collateral. Bovar will see money flowing into his accounts, but not the scale of his exposure on the stock market, nor the true risks of loss.

Financial chaos is certain, and irrevocable.

23

DOUBLE BUBBLE

VASILY VASILIEV STROLLS across his immaculate Surrey lawn. He's entirely unaware of the heady smell of roses that fills the air, the texture of the newly cut grass beneath his beige deck shoes, nor the noise of his teenage children playing in the pool. His nose is down and eyes fixed on the screen of his mobile. It shows the dashboard of diamond production in Bovar's Russian factories.

He swipes to get the price per carat, then quickly calculates the gross profit when the stones hit the market. Even he is impressed. To think they're about to multiply that production at no extra cost!

It's then that the inspiration strikes him: *if the new technology can create perfect layers of diamond, they can cover anything with diamond, right? I'll have to check, but if they can put a diamond layer over a much cheaper stone, it'll become a diamond? Hell, this could really make some money. Diamonds are as good as cash in some parts of the world. Shit, this could be enormous.* Regretfully, he dismisses the calculation, and calls Bychkov. *That arrogant arsehole might not have any imagination, but we're bound as partners ... for now.*

Besides, Bychkov already has factories; Vasiliev's skills lie in trading, particularly with currencies.

The number rings three times before Bychkov answers.

'Uri, I have an idea.'

'Vasily, it's good to hear from you. You've seen the dashboard? Good news, eh?'

The two men pause to congratulate themselves.

'I'm listening,' says Bychkov.

I bet you are, thinks Vasiliev.

'I'm no scientist, but I've read the background documents. Yes, we can make bigger and better diamonds, but I reckon we can also make a cover for other stones. If it walks like a duck and quacks like a duck, it's a duck, right? Our production costs go through the floor and our profits ... think of the profits.'

'You mean use silicon carbide as the core?'

'What? You've already thought of this?'

'Vasily, brother, my factories depend on people who are experts at things I'm not even aware of. Silicon carbide with a diamond coat ...'

Vasiliev feels like his mind is a fountain of

confetti-coloured dollars. He smiles so widely, he can feel the air on his teeth.

'You're sure about this?'

'Everything that is genius is simple,' quotes Bychkov.

'Very true and he who doesn't take risks doesn't drink champagne, my friend.'

'We must go and take a look at our new invention as soon as possible.'

'Friday?'

'There's an airport one hour from the site.'

'Let's take a helicopter together, then a couple of cars. Perhaps we might have lunch before we visit? Our security can drive down separately.'

'Delightful. Until Friday, my friend.'

As Vasiliev lowers his handset, he becomes aware of a tremendous thirst. He sees the housekeeper moving in the house and calls her to bring drinks outside. *It's time for a celebration; good times breed good friends,* he thinks to himself, before another idea comes: *I can buy our manufactured diamonds at cost, then trade them at the market price for mined diamonds. That way I get to launder money and make a profit at the same time. Double bubble.*

24

GOING WELL

Johns feels that the first full day has gone well. The Domino update has gone without a hitch, and the forges are running perfectly. *Why wouldn't they?* he thinks, *They're just glorified microwave ovens. Very expensive ones.* Then he reminds himself of their technical beauty, their precision and what they enable him to achieve.

The lab supply lines are functioning perfectly, and they have enough key materials to run a stress test. All is well. So much so, that he sets the system to run the last Bristol experiment overnight. As good a beginning as can be hoped.

When he and Polly lock up the lab at eight, they're pleasantly surprised at the transformation downstairs in the cottage. The kitchen is clean, tidy and fully stocked, and the air is filled with the delicious aroma of spices and garlic. The meal has come from an Indian restaurant in Bude; a well-thumbed menu remains tacked to the small, grubby noticeboard. Johns touches it as though it were a friendly talisman. He's still standing there when there's a knock on the door.

Ivan is brisk, but clearly proud of his cleaning efforts, and mentions in passing that the kitchen alone took three hours of work for two men.

'You'll have a visitor tomorrow, Professor,' says Ivan.

'Oh?'

'Mr Loge will come here at eleven and will stay for lunch; we're to collect food for you at noon, and bring it here. He'll be accompanied by a third party, to discuss the contract. That's the entire message.'

Johns blinks. 'Thank you for the cleaning, it was quite unnecessary.'

Ivan and Polly exchange a glance that speaks to the contrary.

An hour later, with the remains of supper cleared away, Johns again notes that his assistant seems more relaxed since coming to the cottage. Though she remains taciturn, the atmosphere is easier between them. Like him, she seems genuinely excited at making progress with the work.

'We should discuss the contract,' says Johns.

‘We have to assume the rooms are bugged, Professor.’

‘Of course,’ says Johns, who hasn’t considered this eventuality.

‘I’ve looked around and found a few small devices, but left them in place. I don’t see what use listening tools are unless they’ve got short range Wi-Fi, but then they’d be close enough to hear.’

‘Quite,’ says Johns, perplexed. *No matter,* he thinks.

25

BRISTOL

As Xenia and Saul sit with a cup of tea, the farmhouse kitchen is warmed by both the Aga and the late afternoon sun.

'I'm going to call one of Polly's flatmates,' says Xenia, fiddling nervously with a teaspoon, 'maybe she's got some news.'

The conversation is brief.

'They haven't seen her since first thing Monday morning. She left early. That's Polly, I guess; she likes to keep things to herself.'

'Zee, I'm sure –'

'They checked her room and everything's normal, though some bags are missing. I knew it.'

'We don't know anything, Zee.'

'I hope I'm over-reacting but, if we don't hear anything by morning, would you do me a huge favour?'

'Of course.'

'I'm going to give you Polly's work address. Would you drive to Bristol and say hi?'

'You're really worried, aren't you?'

'I am. I'm very intuitive. I know something's wrong.'

'Sure, if it makes you feel easier. Keep some supper warm for me.'

'Sorry, of course. Call me when you get there, yeah? I'll let them know you're on your way.'

Early the next day, Xenia reports she's barely slept. Her 7 a.m. call to the apartment had only yielded the sleepy voice of one of her flatmates intoning, 'We've still not seen her. No, we don't know of any boyfriend.'

As Saul sets off towards Bristol, heavy skies overhead suggest a break in the long spell of fine weather. The large engine of the bike responds smoothly to the demand for power, as Saul speeds along the straight road west. The smell of hay and grass is a constant note in the cool breeze that rushes through his visor.

He arrives at the labs about nine. As soon as he's dismounted from the bike, packed his gear and checked his hair, the thrill of seeing Polly again grabs him by the entrails.

As he walks into the entranceway, the smell of

the corridors instantly reminds him of the alienation he felt from the realm of science as a schoolboy. It's as though he operates in a different world from the alchemists that work here. An earnest student directs him to Johns' lab where he finds both Lucy and Anna in animated conversation. Saul can't help but notice that, indeed, Johns' lab assistants are good-looking, with open faces and ready smiles. But there is no Polly.

The room is bright and spotlessly clean, with an array of imposing grey-painted and steel high-tech equipment, fed by yellow rubber pipelines, and vented by corrugated aluminium ducts. All of this is so different from the quotidian for Saul. He feels a rush, a nervousness, and defaults to his façade of high intensity investigative reporter.

The girls look up, alarmed.

'Can you tell me where I can find Polly Smith?' he says.

Anna, brushing back a wisp of dark hair from her bob says, 'She's not here.'

'It's important.'

Lucy, pale-skinned, looks embarrassed, 'We can't talk.' She turns away to the papers on the desk in front of her.

'Professor Johns?' asks Saul.

Anna stands now, her chin raised, 'I'm sorry, who are you?'

'A friend.' Saul passes them his press credentials.

'Is something wrong? How do you know about this?' She takes a step forward to inspect the card.

'We know each another socially. Polly's a friend of my sister-in-law and was staying with us this weekend.'

'She told us she was going to see Xenia.' says Anna, visibly relieved.

'Zee was expecting to hear back from Polly about some big work meeting.'

'No meetings here. We had the day off on Monday. Unusual. Very. Especially after last week.'

'What happened on Friday?'

Lucy and Anna look at one another for confirmation. 'We can't talk about it,' says Anna.

'I'm guessing it's really important.'

'We really can't say.'

Saul senses the discomfort in the air, which confirms Xenia's suspicion that the breakthrough is significant.

'Could it be that the professor and Polly are involved with one another? Without you knowing?' he asks.

'No way. Absolutely, no way. She definitely isn't interested in him like that. None of us are. I mean he's brilliant, but ... no way,' replies Anna with brisk confidence.

'Does the university know they're missing?' he asks.

'We called the Head of Sciences office, when the professor didn't come in on Tuesday.'

'Maybe there's someone else who knows where they've gone? Does Professor Johns keep a diary?'

Anna regards him carefully, as though doing a complex mental calculation.

'The logbooks and the back-up hard drives are missing,' she says. 'I'll show you his diary,' and leads the way out of the lab to Johns' office. 'I can get into the uni network from here, and see if he's updated his calendar.' she says.

While Anna logs on, Saul uses the time to survey his surroundings. A man's jacket hangs on the desk chair that Lucy is using. One of the drawers of the desk is slightly open. Somehow, he has to get the room to himself. The phone rings, and Anna picks up.

'No, he's not here. I work with him, can I help?' Saul hears a male voice, talking firmly. 'OK. Yes, I'll ask him to call when he returns.' She puts the receiver down. 'That's a coincidence. It was the uni admin. They don't seem that bothered. They seem to think —.'

'What?'

'Like they were expecting it. I can tell you for sure, we weren't. And we work alongside them every day.'

'Is there a daybook for progress in the lab?'

'Everything goes into the terminals, of course.

We normally keep the logbooks in here as a safety. We keep notes for the previous seven days.'

'Could I see last week's?' Saul asks, hoping they're back in the lab rather than here. Lucy leaves to collect them. He scoots around to the jacket and rifles the pockets, where he finds a slim notebook. He checks the drawers; all, almost completely empty. At the back of one, he finds a black USB stick. That follows the notebook into his jeans, just as he hears Lucy's footsteps in the corridor outside.

The extreme technical convolutions of the weekly report leaves him none the wiser. Ten minutes later, Saul is back outside, with the familiar rush of adrenaline he feels when a story begins to open itself to him. His disappointment on missing Polly is now countered by the excitement of checking the contents of the flash drive and notebook. *Xenia's right: something's awry.* He's in two minds. As a journalist, he's trained to ask the right questions and analyse the data. As a man, he wants Polly to know he cares.

He just makes it back, before the skies open with grey rods of blurred rain. They spit and hiss on the summer lawn. It releases tension in the atmosphere after the previous ten days of continuous hot, dry weather. But a familiar anxiety is building in Saul's belly.

Xenia's out. The USB is unreadable on his machine. He sends the data packet to Michael, his one-man tech team, who's accustomed to Saul dropping mysterious files for no apparent reason. Michael doesn't seem to have a social life, and understands the confidential nature of the journalist's work. This perhaps explains why he treats everything Saul sends him as both urgent and important.

Saul gets a ping confirming receipt just moments later.

The pocket notebook contains pages of algebra, a flow chart of symbols headed with the letters FTA, a list of home improvements, and a handful of names. He begins trying to decode each page. He's at a loss with the maths, so emails Michael images of the calculations, together with the flow chart. Perhaps his numbers-oriented mind will make sense where Saul sees only an impenetrable code. Then he recognizes a trick used by Leonardo da Vinci; what he thought was part of an equation might be reversed in a mirror. With the help of an online dictionary, Saul deciphers L-O-G-E. The letters are in Cyrillic, which points to Johns having a knowledge of Slav culture. According to his profile on the university website, Professor Johns has studied in Moscow. *That word LOGE ... it's familiar,* thinks Saul.

None of the names in the notebook register as significant. The list of home improvements is even less edifying, although the large generator obviously isn't for Johns' Bristol flat. The flow chart makes no sense to Saul; an online search offers him Free Trade Agreement, Freestyle Trampolining Association ... but he knows that the symbols hold the key to unlock the meaning.

The reverberation from the heavy farmhouse door downstairs tells him that Xenia is back.

He tucks the notebook into a drawer, and hopes that Michael will come up with something. Saul can feel the darkness of ignorance crowding in around him, and he doesn't try to deny it. It's always like this in the early stages of an investigation, when nothing is known. This time there's someone he likes in the firing line, and that makes all the difference.

26

LUNCH WITH LOGE

Johns and Polly prepare the sitting room for the occasion. The round, battered Georgian drop-leaf table, together with four upright chairs of dubious vintage, are cleared of books and newspapers, and moved near the window. The two armchairs and a sofa, in ragged chintz covers, are pressed more closely around the small wood-burning stove. The room is pleasantly cool, and a gentle breeze wafts through the open window. A chipped oriental vase of tiny wild flowers is on the shelf over the fireplace. The day is so bright outside that anything in shadow within the house – like the forlorn rugs – is entirely hidden. Even the mantles in the gas lights have been replaced with fresh, white gauze.

As is his habit, Loge arrives punctually for the eleven o'clock meeting. The smaller figure of the Accountant follows in his wake, dressed in his customary grey suit. If possible, his pallor is more pronounced in daylight, with his long face and sad eyes giving him the air of an undertaker on a bad day.

Polly has opted for a short, pale-blue skirt and a thin blouse which, when she comes down to open the door for the guests, strikes the Accountant dumb. Johns, when he sees her, goes into a mild coughing fit. After the initial introductions, he disappears into the kitchen to emerge soon after with a tray of espressos. Their surfaces tremble slightly, as he places them onto the table. 'I have a new coffee pot, perfect for my gas hob,'he declares with an expectant look, as each takes a conspicuously appreciative sip.

'Your cottage is delightful,' says Loge, keen to get down to business.

'Thank you,' says Johns. 'It's all thanks to Polly. A transformation. I barely recognize my own home.'

Preliminaries over, the four go through the contract, line by line, under the firm control of the Accountant. As a result, the agonizing analysis is drawn out longer than necessary. Loge concludes that the Accountant's soul must have shrivelled by continuous exposure to numbers, abstracted from any life they represent.

They adjourn for lunch.

Bovar had insisted champagne be bought for his new creatures and yet, Loge observes, it's the Accountant who feels obliged to drink nine-tenths of it. Polly takes the merest sip. The more the

Accountant consumes, the more he talks, seemingly determined to convince the party that he is both fascinating and powerful. The peak of his monologue comes when he declares, 'Of course, if you hadn't accepted ...' before tailing off, embarrassed.

Loge doesn't drink, and feels that it's dishonourable to mix alcohol with a business negotiation, despite his employer viewing it as an obvious tactic of warfare. He knows Johns is teetotal, so ordered an additional bottle of non-alcoholic wine. Besides, Loge wants Johns coherent. After lunch, the Accountant rests back with a satisfied sigh, his indiscretion temporarily forgotten by him. He allows Loge the enormous privilege of covering the remaining points. This takes a remarkably short period of time.

'Finally, your public tribute,' announces Loge. 'This is, as I believe it's called, the elephant in the room, no? Unfortunately, due to your abrupt departure from the university, you will not be able to work in the UK again. Certainly not in academia.' He leaves a respectful pause, to allow the full impact to land. Johns nods gravely; Polly barely registers. 'We know, from an inside source, the university has now contacted the sponsors. They have raised the issue with MI6, who will no doubt take control of the investigation.' Loge examines his hands. 'This is a complication we foresaw and, therefore, will increase your protection here. It does, however, mean that your names will not be published, and it's therefore solely a matter of securing the discretion of your professional colleagues. Do you have any questions?'

Polly smiles enigmatically; Johns has begun to perspire.

'Are Lucy and Anna safe?' he asks.

'Good heavens, yes!' replies Loge.

'We just need to ensure they respect your decision,' offers the Accountant, giving no comfort to anyone.

There is a long silence. For some reason, Loge finds himself thinking of his wife and realizes he hasn't contacted her since arriving in Britain. He's not even thought of her, let alone of buying that new dress she was insisting on. He continues, 'You have my personal guarantee that I will do everything in my power to ensure your extraordinary work will be put in front of the Nobel committee, and any other awards you nominate. At a later date we will discuss your living arrangements. Given the involvement of MI6, it would obviously be wise for you to leave the UK for a time. One additional matter, which I must address with you, is that your new guardians are coming to visit.'

Johns, who had appeared to enter a reverie, at the mention of international awards, sits bolt upright in surprise. 'What is this? What do you mean?'

'My employer, Mr Bovar, has granted the

exclusive licence to operate global diamond manufacturing to two gentlemen, resident in England. They will visit your home ' – Loge checks his watch – ' in half an hour.'

'But I wasn't notified,' stutters Johns.

'No, indeed,' continues Loge. 'Nor was I until this morning.'

'This is most improper,' says Johns, getting to his feet. 'I can't simply be passed from hand to hand like a piece of meat in a butcher's shop.'

Loge raises both palms placatingly. 'There is no question of that. These gentlemen are as enthusiastic, if not more so, than my employer, to see that you succeed. They will do everything in their power to ensure you're happy in your work, and that it bears the fruit we all so earnestly hope for.'

Johns leaves the room muttering, 'I need more coffee.' Loge raises his eyebrows towards Polly. She goes to join Johns, and returns with him soon after.

'If it must be, it must be,' says Johns. 'Am I to know the names of my new owners?'

'They do not own you, my friend. They have merely procured the licence to use your invention.'

'Yes, yes,' says Johns, clearly upset. Polly looks at him comfortingly, and it pacifies him. Loge notes this new dynamic, of which he'd not been previously aware.

27

THE VISIT

RAIN LASHES THE FARMHOUSE WINDOWS, as the glowering sky continues to release its burden onto the still-parched landscape. Despite the downpour, the air remains heavy with apathetic torpor, smothering whatever hope or inspiration Xenia and Saul try to kindle in one another.

'I'll send Polly another message,' says Xenia.

'Telegram?'

'I'm using everything. I just want to know she's safe. Albie called earlier, and was as concerned as me.'

Saul's convinced that Albie would be laid back about Polly's disappearance, but would have hated hearing Xenia in distress. 'We'll reach her. I'm sure she's OK. Lunch? My turn.' He immediately starts taking food out of the fridge.

Xenia is head down, typing on her phone, when

a nondescript, dark saloon pulls up outside. The back doorbell rings. 'I'll get it,' he says.

At the door, a man and a woman huddle under a small black umbrella. Jehovah's Witnesses, thinks Saul. He greets them with a smile, to hide his irritation.

The male is crammed into his dark blue suit and tie. His torso seems composed of two solid brick cubes, placed one above the other, with a smaller cube on top for the head, crowned with thick, curling black hair. His brow is furrowed and heavy, and green, photochromic lenses obscure his eyes. His hands are square and strong, but his fingernails neatly shaped. The whole effect is of a man weighed down by mighty problems, but bearing up with indomitable will.

His companion has the bearing of a junior school headteacher at the height of her career and, compared with her colleague, seems placid and gentle. She wears a short, light grey coat showing a dark red blouse beneath. Her light brown hair is swept back into a tight ponytail, emphasizing the polished skin of her forehead. Her eyes sparkle with intelligence, but the tension around her eyes and mouth tells of conflict.

'Mr Danver?' she asks.

'Perhaps you want my brother.'

'Mr Saul Danver?'

A cold chill runs down Saul's back. 'Is Albie,

OK? I mean Albert? My brother?' The memory of that call to the hospital on a heavy, wet winter's day when his father had died, comes flooding into his mind. He dismisses it immediately. *Not now, Saul*, he tells himself.

'It's about your recent visit to Bristol,' she answers. 'We have some questions.'

'Regarding what?' Every fibre of Saul's professional being bridles at this invasion of his privacy.

'We're from MI6,' says the man, deadpan, using a verbal crowbar.

'May I see your credentials?' Saul recognizes them as authentic. 'Xenia, we have visitors,' he says, walking ahead of the uninvited guests to the kitchen.

'My name is Finch, Julia Finch,' says the woman, emphasizing her first name. 'And this is my colleague, Paresh Kapoor.'

Mr Kapoor makes a valiant attempt at a smile, and shows a set of alarmingly small teeth, which gives the impression of small dog patiently awaiting a treat. His lenses have normalized now, and Saul sees the eager concentration in the dark eyes behind them.

'I can see you're about to eat, so we won't waste your time,' says Finch. 'We're interested in the whereabouts of Professor Dmitri Johns, for whom your friend Polly Smith works.'

'I don't know him, Mrs Finch,' replies Xenia.

The woman remains still and silent and staring. Saul recognizes it as his own favoured tactic to provoke subjects into talking. Xenia doesn't comply.

'Please call me Julia. You do know Polly Smith?'

'We're old friends. We were at university together.'

'Professor Johns is involved with sensitive work at his laboratories,' continues Julia. 'We've established —'

'He's not what he says he is,' interrupts Kapoor. 'He's been working on the dark web with unsavoury characters. We're not interested in your friend, but we must talk with Johns. If you know anything, please tell us now.'

Kapoor is nothing, if not direct. If Julia Finch is disturbed by the interruption, she doesn't show it. Again, they leave a yawning silence and, as before, neither Xenia nor Saul volunteer information.

'We know you went to Bristol yesterday, and visited Materials and Sciences.' says Finch, turning to Saul, 'We've talked with Lucy and Anna and they passed your contact details on to us. The university has officially notified Johns and Smith as missing persons, and we're leading the inquiry. Professor Johns has been on our radar for some time.'

Xenia breaks her silence. 'Is Polly in danger?'

'Not as far as we're aware, but we need your help,' says Kapoor, eyeing Saul. 'Any information you can give will be valuable, and ensure your friend's safe return.'

'Of course,' responds Saul. 'Lucy and Anna blinded me with science, and I left none the wiser. I met Polly for the first time this weekend.'

'You're an experienced journalist, Mr Danver. You know how to gather facts.' Both Finch and Kapoor now fix their eyes on him. Saul has long since mastered the poker face. Another time-out. He breathes deeply and calmly, smiling inscrutably.

Julia Finch breaks the spell. 'Very good. Just to let you know we're actively searching for your friend.' Her look lingers on Saul, before turning to Xenia. 'We believe she and Johns left at the same time. Together. Please let us know if you have any communication of any kind with either of the parties. We'll leave now.'

Xenia sees them to the door. It's stopped raining. As they leave, Kapoor turns to face her.

'You've recently started using Telegram.'

'Yes,' says Xenia, looking genuinely surprised.

'Yes,' says Kapoor, waiting a beat before stepping away. Together, he and Julia Finch return to their black saloon and depart, driving very, very slowly.

'Well, that was strange,' says Xenia, looking at the umbrella, left behind like a discarded toy.

'They've been watching me for the past twenty-four hours and I didn't notice.'

'They're professionals,' Xenia shrugs.

'So am I.'

'You know what I mean. What have you found out?'

'Nothing yet, Zee, but I will. I promise.'

Xenia checks her handset which she'd slipped into her trouser pocket as soon as she saw Saul with guests. Saul sees her shoulders, initially hunched and tense, suddenly drop.

'Polly's been in touch ... she's fine ... it seems she needed a few days' holiday.'

'I don't understand,' says Saul. 'We've had MI6 in your home searching for a rogue scientist, Polly and Johns disappear at the same time, and she didn't call when she said she would. Now you're not worried?'

She hesitates, then turns the phone to show him the screen: *With Father in Cornwall. Complicated.*

'Father? I thought her family were all in Estonia,' says Saul.

A long, sad look from Xenia, and then, 'She's pregnant. It's complicated.'

Inside, Saul aches with disappointment, but says nothing.

28

TENSION RISES

SAUL HAS SPENT time formulating a story on Etique, but keeps coming to the conclusion that it is a seedy little scam, run by a couple of greedy, bourgeois, small-time crooks. Yes, people are getting ripped off, but there's no geopolitical angle or broader story. The paper would laugh at him for exposing a little business on the make, however corrupt.

The question that keeps bubbling up in his mind is, *What's Bovar doing with industrial diamond manufacturing? If he's the crook I think he is ...*

The visit by MI6 is of more immediate concern; *it shows Johns is involved with something of national, perhaps international, importance. Interesting.*

His mobile rings.

'Michael, here.' The reedy tone, slight lisp and hesitancy of the caller, all speak of a man who finds interpersonal communication excruciatingly hard to negotiate.

'Michael, you're a star. Did you crack it?'

'No problem. Well, I say that, Saul. It wasn't easy because ...'

Saul thinks it merciful to head Michael off, before he gets the full technical breakdown. 'Michael, it's me, remember? The thick one, who thinks a kernel panic is a military disaster.'

Michael rewards Saul's technical joke with an involuntary snort of laughter. 'Well, a kernel panic ...'

'What's on the USB, Mike?'

'Oh, yes. It's about six months old. It looks like one programme, but it's two. The main programme is for manufacturing something, but I can be more specific about the other. There's a reference to the FTA.'

'Sure. What about it?'

'My guess, it's the FTSE All-World stock index. I think the sub-programme trades stocks or financial products. The flow chart in the notes was the clue I needed.'

'It came from a materials science laboratory.'

'Well, the main programme is almost certainly for manufacturing a novel material, but the sub is something else. This isn't the result of a weekend hobby-coding; it's deep and well-disguised. The version you sent me isn't complete.'

. . .

Hours later, Saul and Xenia are sitting down for supper. Albie's flight is delayed.

Xenia looks down at her plate, 'I can't eat.'

'I know, Zee. I'm worried too. I wasn't going to tell you, but I took a notebook from Professor Johns' study at the university.'

'Saul! You haven't?! That's great.'

'Yeah, but if anyone asks, you don't know about it, OK?'

'So what have you found?'

'There's a reference to a guy named Loge. I've found him online, and he's Bovar's technical director.'

'Who's Bovar?'

Xenia had gone straight to the question that Saul wanted to avoid, at least until Albie returned. It was too late; she could look it up as easily as anyone.

'Maxim Bovar, head of the eponymous Bovar Industries. Into manufacturing on a giant scale and one of the richest men in Russia; military hardware, industrial diamond manufacturing, diamond mining and much more. He's been a huge beneficiary from the break-up of the Soviet Union, when the state had a collective heart attack in the early nineties.'

'I was barely born then, Saul. Why do I get the feeling that this is bad news?'

Simon pauses. 'I believe Bovar Industries are also behind the mine attacks I was investigating for the paper. He's got a private militia, which he uses to enforce his business interests. A problem with the suppliers? Call in the army. A disagreement over a contract? Call in the army. A dissatisfied customer? Call in the army.'

Xenia laughs involuntarily. 'I don't believe you. Saul, this is mad. No wonder the paper doesn't want to print this.'

Saul doesn't respond. He just sits, gently watching, as she dissolves into tears.

Albie's plane is delayed and delayed and delayed. Saul puts a DVD on to distract Xenia, but she constantly checks the online arrivals' board via an app. Her husband finally walks through the door at one-fifteen.

'Everybody up? Let's party!' he says, with forced jollity. He looks wiped.

After the initial hugs, Xenia says the words she's been saying to herself all evening, 'Polly's been taken by international gangsters.'

29

WRONG HANDS

THE CRUNCH of tyres on loose stones announces the arrival of three identical black BMW 7 series at the cottage. Out of each, almost in unison, step several tall, lean men in dark sunglasses and over-tight black T-shirts. They bristle with tension, and spread out to scan the terrain.

Within, Johns cranes his neck to see who's arrived, 'They've brought more goons,' he says to no-one in particular, 'What is it with these people?' His squinting has been metronomic since Loge's revelation of the new owners. The Accountant, nominally in control during the contractual discussions, is twisting his hands anxiously. Polly sits stock still, watching Johns.

Two of the minders go to the rear doors of the leading cars and open them ceremoniously. Loge knows he must reassure both Johns and Polly,

'They're taking you seriously. Take it as a compliment. You're very important to them.' He's determined to maintain his connection with Johns, despite the shift of power taking place.

The serpentine figure of Uri Bychkov unwinds from the first car, just as the second yields the altogether more agile form of Vasily Vasiliev. 'Fucking *poyezdka uzhasnyy* ... terrible trip,' he says, blinking in the fierce light of the early afternoon that blazes full on the modest cottage. He swats at the gathering of midges, attracted by the exotic oil he uses to stimulate growth in his thinning hair.

Loge steps out of the room to open the front door, just as one of the acolytes does the same from the other side. There's a moment of confusion, before Bychkov and Vasiliev stride into the house. Loge introduces himself. Bychkov's handshake is almost wet, telling of nothing. Vasiliev has a fierce grasp, turning Loge's hand below his and energetically pumping, eyes almost bulging, as they stare him out.

Johns welcomes the two businessmen warily into his low-ceilinged sitting room. Vasiliev eyes the exposed beams and proclaims it 'charming', while Bychkov makes no attempt to conceal his disdain at the sight of the faded curtains, the worn seats of the old armchairs and the burn marks on the rug in front of the fireplace. It's only when his eyes light on the vase of wild flowers picked by Polly, that he finds the energy to declaim, 'Splendid. May I?' He plucks the white and blue porcelain from the shelf and turns it in his hand, noting the brushwork of the characters on the base. 'Very nice. Japanese arita-ware, late nineteenth century.' He arranges his features into a languid smile and stretches out a long, thin hand to greet Johns. Simultaneously, Vasiliev activates his face, showing his perfect white teeth. He bows before Polly with practised charm.

'And who are you?' Bychkov asks the Accountant, who is over-lubricated by champagne, and perspiring profusely, despite the cool inside the cottage.

'I personally oversee all contracts in the UK for Maxim Bovar.'

'Then we won't need you. Feel free to leave. Now,' says Vasiliev, nodding.

Loge shrugs, and the Accountant gathers his papers to wait outside.

Johns immediately launches into a shopping list, detailing specific machinery he requires for the advancement of his work. Vasiliev cracks his knuckles in impatience, then raises one hand and says, 'We'll come to this. Can we first see this wonderful invention?'

Johns smiles at the flattery and opens his laptop at the sign-in screen for Domino.

The two guests look at one another in dismay. 'Is this it? We have driven across Britain to see your laptop?' Bychkov asks.

Loge steps in hastily. 'No indeed, gentlemen. The manufacturing is highly advanced technology; the laboratory is outside. The factories, which I understand you've recently acquired, have the facilities to exploit Professor Johns' extraordinary work.'

Relief is evident on both guests faces.

'How long might that take, incidentally?' asks Vasiliev.

Loge pauses, knowing that the factories already have all the gases, minerals and equipment needed. At Bovar's insistence, they started running the new process, within hours of the download. Domino is already in play, 'A matter of weeks.' In truth, he expected definite results within twenty-four hours.

Vasieliev's eyes are shining with excitement, 'Excellent.'

Loge notes that whilst Johns has masked his acute anxiety, he has a look of utter disgust with his guests.

'First, I must I ask you to take ownership,' says Loge hurriedly. 'I need you to enter some personal details, and we also need a proof of identity.'

Johns attaches a fingerprint scanner for biometric confirmation. Bychkov narrows his eyes and, for a moment, it looks like the two men understand one another perfectly. Mutual loathing.

With all details entered, Bychkov asks, 'OK, is that it?'

'One more thing,' says Johns. 'We have to secure it onto the blockchain.'

'What is this blockchain?' asks Vasiliev.

Johns looks nervously at Loge, who interprets. 'The blockchain is a distributed public ledger of all transactions. Indestructible.'

'Speak English or Russian. Be clear, man.'

'It's a highly secure, digital contract that permanently and indelibly records your ownership online. It requires an internet connection. Unfortunately, there is no access from the cottage, but it's available a short walk from here.'

Bychkov is astonished, 'You can't be serious.'

Loge opens his hands in supplication.

'Of course, we'll wait,' Vasiliev says, lest his partner spoil the moment with a tirade.

Johns gathers his laptop and mobile and, together with Loge, leaves the cottage. 'It shouldn't take more than twenty minutes,' he says, leaving Polly to play the part of hostess. Vasiliev indicates for two of the blackshirts to follow the men.

They pass the Accountant, sitting in Loge's hire car. He looks like a little boy left out of a party.

Shortly after reaching the brow of the valley, they hear men's voices shouting from the direction of the cottage.

'What is it? Is Polly all right with these people?' asks Johns, clearly terrified.

'No doubt she is safe, my friend,' says Loge. 'I

suspect our security team have met their bodyguards.'

Returning, they find that the remaining blackshirts have retreated to their vehicles. The Accountant is cowering in Loge's car, and Sokolov, the head of the original security detail, stands by the doorway.

'We had a problem with the visitors' bodyguards.' says Sokolov, glaring at their escort, 'They didn't know their place.'

'So you attract attention?' asks Loge with disdain.

'I'm sorry for the disturbance; they were indiscreet. We don't need unwanted guests.'

Loge gently places a reassuring hand between Johns' shoulders to steer him back into the house. As they enter, it's clear to see that Vasiliev is more captivated by Polly's legs than he is about the finer points of Johns' work.

'OK, we're done,' says Loge. 'Now the tour.'

Johns leads Bychkov and Vasiliev back into the bright sunlight, and on to the outbuilding. Uncharacteristically, Bychkov is the first to give a gasp of astonishment at the array of technology behind the padlocked door.

'How does this all work?' asks Vasiliev.

Again, Loge answers. 'The metadata you've entered generates an anonymous token – a unique code – and links you exclusively to the manufacturing in a facility like this. Your new factories, on activating the programme, will become party to your side of the contract.'

As Johns describes each stage of the miracle that transforms gas into a diamond, he loses his inhibitions. He now seems delighted to guide the newcomers through the mysteries of his domain. To a scientist like Loge, it's a fascinating insight into the mind of a genius; very hard to follow, but deeply rewarding. However, he recognizes the guests just want evidence of large and apparently expensive pieces of machinery; they have no interest in, or understanding of, the process. He sees them stifle yawns through gritted teeth.

The tour complete, Johns releases them back to the cottage. The sitting room seems several degrees cooler to Loge. It may be their retreat from the heat, but the visitors' menace seems to have diminished.

'One word before we leave,' says Bychkov, looking directly at Johns. 'We've invested a great deal of money into this venture and expect results. You do understand?'

Johns nods, but his cheek resumes its twitch.

Vasiliev picks up the baton. 'We will be very, very generous to you when we succeed. This will be in addition to whatever Maxim Bovar pays you. However, should any element fail, we will be absolutely ruthless,' he pauses, 'We expect perfection.'

He then turns abruptly to Loge.

'You will remain our liaison on all technical matters, that is correct?' A faint tone of respect in his voice.

'I will be in the country for perhaps two more weeks, then fly back to Russia.'

'I see,' said Bychkov, 'we're putting our people on the ground here for enhanced security of the genius and his estimable research partner.' He smiles at Johns with all the charm of a tiger that's trapped a gazelle. 'Our people will work alongside Bovar's for the immediate future. Perhaps you would invite the head of your security detail to join us?'

Loge goes to the front door and finds Sokolov, who has remained on duty there. 'Thank you for joining us,' continues Bychkov. 'Your team are to work hand in glove with our security detail, to protect these most valuable of assets.' He nods deferentially at Johns and Polly.

Sokolov has anticipated this, 'I've been in touch with my commander. Mr Bovar suggests that you call him direct if you're unhappy with the present arrangement.'

The silence in the room becomes as heavy as the slate floors and granite walls, bearing down with an intense, immovable pressure. Vasiliev and Bychkov exchange a glance.

Bychkov speaks. 'If anything ... anything' he repeats, looking directly into Sokolov's eyes, 'happens to impede the work of Professor Johns and Miss Smith, I hold you personally responsible. Do you understand me?'

Despite Bychkov's threat, Sokolov seems unmoved and, below the low ceiling, appears to tower over him. 'Certainly sir', he replies, in measured tones.

Bychkov turns to face the professor. 'Thank you for your hospitality.'

With this, the two men return to their cars and, wheels spitting dirt and stone, depart. They take with them the squad of five, unsmiling men and one woman, who have had to reload their luggage of identical backpacks and assorted flight cases.

Sokolov, Loge, Johns and Polly watch the trail of dust from the cars fade on the gentle breeze, and a new bond of unity envelops them.

'What does this mean?' asks Polly.

'It means your visitors don't want anyone to get their hands on your innovation,' says Loge. 'You have my number. Please call if there's any difficulty.'

'It's important you're involved,' says Johns.

'I remain your liaison in all technical matters, and my word has not changed. I will do everything in my power to ensure you get full recognition among the global scientific community. Good luck, Johns. Polly.' Loge pauses for a moment, inspecting her face, to reassure himself about the past connection. *Perhaps she is a dvojnik … a double. It's nine years since I last saw her; I could be mistaken.* He resolves to tackle her directly about this on his next visit. *Not today.*

30

EYE IN THE SKY

Kapoor and Finch sit, side by side, in the stalls of the enormous, darkened gallery of the Hub, situated deep in the air-conditioned bowels of MI6. What light there is, emanates from communications desk panels, large suspended screens and their own laptops. Here, anything in the world that is monitored electronically – outside buildings and in – may be analysed and presented as graphics, video and audio.

Here, Paresh Kapoor feels more at home, more connected, than anywhere. He's spent ten years of his life monitoring the dark web. No matter how many times he sees scams, terror images and drug trades online, they never fail to pain him. The fact this sick domain prospers is way out of his or anyone else's control; at least working in the physical world offers him some promise of intervention and resolution. That's why he transferred out of cyber-surveillance into operations. Kapoor's comfort with technology also enables him to grasp the basis of Johns' materials' work at the university.

Julia Finch, with first class degrees in both Classics and Mathematics from Cambridge, freely admits to Kapoor she's only happy to go to the 'dismal' Hub for a good internet connection.

MI6 had registered the professor on their database when he returned from his studies in Moscow. Now their fears are justified. Satellite images show activity at his cottage on the North Cornwall coast, close to Comms West. This poses a double problem for Finch and Kapoor, as even the locals who work there don't know the true purpose of 'the military base'.

In 2013, a whistleblower shone a searchlight on mass surveillance conducted by the UK and USA. He revealed the digital little secret, that every citizen's email, phone call, social media post and direct message is collected, processed and stored. All the time. CommsWest is a crucial node in the network: a critical listening station.

A layer of satellite monitoring data reveals a definite heat bloom from Johns' outbuilding; massively different when compared with the cottage. Something is at work in there. There are several sets of images, the most recent showing activity following the visit from three black saloon cars – corroborated from the base as BMWs – and the dispersal of a group to set up what looks like a security cordon.

Attempts to infiltrate the area near the cottage have not been fruitful. Several two-person teams, masquerading as walkers along the coast path, have got within eight hundred metres of Johns' cottage. Each time, large men in dark glasses have materialized, to shadow their every move. A more covert, night-time approach triggered a loud alarm and a hasty retreat.

Finch glances at her laptop and coughs in obvious aversion. 'I've got an email from White Diamonds. Apparently, the university has just told them that Johns is missing. They've referred them to us. Something extra to deal with.'

'We've got too much to do as it is,' mutters Kapoor. 'We've got an intercept on all comms in and out of the cottage, but there's no broadband there, and no mobile signal for us or them. Latest satellite data shows ...'

Julia's face remains inscrutable, as she continues to read, almost absent-mindedly. 'They say they'll put their own team on it if we don't have a result in forty-eight hours. We're going to have to meet with them; they're too powerful to ignore. They go on to say they've contacted their "parliamentary representatives". Oh, really.' She snorts in disgust.

'Julia, we have enough to move in. Johns is

definitely at the cottage and there's at least one person with him. It must be Polly Smith.'

'You're right, of course, but we don't know why Johns has changed course. He's not likely to tell. The university can give him a smack on the wrist, but it's not going to help us. We need a smoking gun.'

'You're convinced he's turned?'

Finch swivels in her chair, to look directly at Kapoor. She smiles, 'Either that or he's on a dirty weekend with a lot of people watching. They've got guards. It's risky.'

'So we wait?'

'This could take weeks. Let's go home. There's nothing more we can do here,' she says, folding her desk Filofax, and stuffing it into an oversize shoulder bag.

Her mobile rings, routed through her laptop, and she puts an earpiece in, moving her mouth close to the microphone. She glances up at Paresh.

'Danver,' she mouths.

It's a break from protocol to receive calls in the Hub, but there's no audio broadcast in the room at present.

'Xenia Danver here. I've heard from Polly.'

'Hi Xenia, Julia here. Thanks for calling. Is she back in Bristol?'

'No. I'm going to read you the message: *With Father in Cornwall. Complicated.*'

'Is that it? When did you get this? No address?'

'I hoped you might know where she is. I'm so worried about her.'

'I'm sure she's fine. We're grateful for your call. Please sit tight, and let us know if you hear more.'

Julia Finch replaces her mobile on the desk. 'Smith has made a call. Why aren't we monitoring her phone?'

'We do. She must have another ... and she must be out of the cottage.'

'Grab your swimsuit, Paresh. We're off to Cornwall. Now.'

31

LOSSES

Vasily Vasiliev is unusual. He abandoned his family in 1983, at the age of fifteen, and took the name of his beloved babushka: Vasilisa. Even now he both detests and loves his long-dead parents. When he left home to fight, his battle was not in uniform in Afghanistan, but on the streets of Moscow. A tumult of emotion never gave him pause. He created his extraordinary business empire from graft, guile and total commitment.

It had initially amused him that Bychkov, the scion of a great Russian family, was named 'Yuri' or 'farmer'. Bychkov had never done a day's physical work in his life. Vasily had sweated and strained as a labourer on building sites, until he found a better way to accumulate wealth: other people's money.

Vasily's personal charm and devotion to his work allowed him to build a reputation as someone who could be trusted to make a profit. He became a trader, and his cut of the payback paved the road to riches. He would do anything to protect a client's interests. Anything.

The collapse of the Soviet Union in 1991 had been a boon to men like Vasiliev. The subsequent privatization of industries allowed the new shareholders to plunder what had previously been State-owned. And some did. By his early 20s Vasily had accumulated a roster of very interesting patrons. But by the mid-nineties, other important people started asking where the money had gone. Awkward. That's when Bovar became a client. The cash needed to leave Russia fast. Switzerland offered the required anonymity, but Vasiliev's clients wanted more: to both launder the money and then invest it, preferably without the inconvenience of taxes.

The young entrepreneur grasped the opportunity.

London offered the means to set up untraceable shell companies, without the hassle of verifying the identity of unnamed beneficiaries. Vasily then established a ladder of multiple destinations that ensured no-one could follow the money. The 'pliable jurisdictions' of UK offshore tax havens, like the Virgin Islands, Cayman Islands, Bermuda, Jersey and Anguilla did the rest. With an alleged tax revenue of seventy-five billion pounds, coming from London's financial services, the UK politicians turned a blind eye. The UK-Russia Cultural Alliance grew in strength, and the Russian laundromat remained in business.

Vasily played a modest part in all of this, but it had made him a very rich man. People needed help and he provided it. He had seldom needed to resort to violence; merely maintaining his own small, highly trained, private militia seemed to have been sufficient.

His most recent reinvention is as an English country gentleman, replete with tweed jackets, corduroy trousers and shooting parties. His office is a London mews house. He's on his way there now, walking briskly, in the balmy summer air, through the quaint, little backstreets of Kensington, just a few days after his visit to Cornwall with Bychkov.

But Vasily is not happy ... not as a man with the promise of an abundantly profitable, new enterprise should be. He's spent an hour and a half searching for missing funds this morning. It revealed nothing. He has a call coming up with Bychkov, and can smell danger. He feels that someone is double-crossing him, and is sure that he knows who.

Vasiliev passes under the archway, leading into the mews, and enters the pink, ivy-clad cottage directly ahead of him. He nods at his PA, and accepts the first double espresso of the day. Within minutes he's on the call.

'Are you good, Uri?' he asks.

'Yes, splendid, splendid. How is it with you, Vasily?' responds Bychkov.

'These are interesting times we live in.'

'Yes, yes, tell me, how are your businesses faring?'

This is all Vasily needs to hear. He is certain Bychkov is goading him. 'Tell me, have you seen the increase in diamond production? Loge is doing an excellent job of bringing the factories online, eh?'

'So it seems. Our timing is good with the price of diamonds rising,' says Bychkov. 'This is nothing to do with the factories, but still ...'

'Things are looking rosy, aye?' says Vasily.

'Indeed ...'

Vasily feels the blood in his temples throbbing stronger with every second. *If Bychkov had complained, we'd be in a difficult situation together but, if everything is fine with him, then it looks bad for me.*

Vasiliev is now convinced that Bychkov has hacked into his account. Both he and Bychkov have teams of cyber warriors to complement their private militia, but Bychkov's is more extensive. Vasily feels a fool not to have seen it immediately. At that moment, red anger floods him, infusing him with energy and determination. *I will destroy Bychkov. This is war.*

. . .

Bychkov knows Vasiliev detests his so-called bourgeois values, but this means nothing to him. If anything, it looks like a vulnerability, which he can use to provoke and manipulate his partner. Besides, how can it be an error to despise the values of the rich and the powerful? As one who has grown up nestled in the bosom of a great family, and then nurtured at the teat of the finest schools available, Bychkov knows the system works. *Simply and perfectly. Those who are rich are the natural rulers, and the weak are subordinate. This is the natural order of things. To disrupt that is to go against the one immutable law: the supremacy of the right. It's obvious the poor should supply. Well,* he admits, *perhaps 'supply' is not the correct word; 'surrender' may be more appropriate. Yes, Vasiliev is rich, but it's new money, not old.*

Similarly, the notion of giving to the public is abhorrent to him. He detests the strictures of living as a patriot in Moscow, and resents the continual haemorrhage of tax roubles from his family to the Duma: it suggests his bloodline is a mere vassal of the State.

Besides, what does Vasiliev make? Nothing. He's merely a money-changer. What good is that to anyone? Apart from when Bychkov Enterprises needs their services, he accepts ... *Governments call people like Vasiliev 'productive' because they can measure the tax take. At least I, Uri Bychkov, can hold my head high knowing that we manufacture useful goods. Mainly. Yet now we are strange bedfellows, Vasiliev and I, brought together by that uneducated pig, Bovar. At least it's yielding the welcome addition of a diamond-manufacturing cartel.*

But Bychkov is equally suspicious. He too has inspected his accounts, and seen unexplained falls. It's obvious from the call that Vasiliev is in good humour. Who else but Vasiliev is in a position to exploit his banking access? Bychkov doesn't know how, but feels certain that this cretin is up to something. He sees no solution other than to seize Vasiliev's position as quickly as possible, and the only way to do that effectively is to exterminate him.

Vermin, he thinks, with disgust.

What he does not concede is that his street-fighting business partner need only rely on himself if his empire crashes. Bychkov, however, has inherited both wealth and factories, *Which I must protect; for my family and for my honour.*

32

THREATS

It is Friday, just a week after the visit from Bychkov and Vasiliev. Polly and Johns have established a working rhythm, and Johns is delighted with their progress.

There is a knock on the outbuilding door. Sokolov, incongruous in a pair of over-designed blue sunglasses and, despite the heat, a chocolate brown wind-cheater.

'Can you come to the house, sir? And you too, miss?'

Underlying the politesse of the invitation is a definite note of authority.

They enter the sitting room to find one of Bychkov and Vasiliev's goons. He is gaunt and sallow, and stands brooding by the fireplace; his uniform black T-shirt and black jeans hang loosely from his frame. For all that, his forearm muscles ripple like a sheaf of wire cables under strain.

For some reason the acrid smell of soot is stronger in here today.

On the small coffee table there are matchsticks, laid head to foot in parallel lines, one inch apart. A tiny pile of white crystals sits at one end.

'What is this? Why is our work being interrupted?' demands Johns.

'Please sit down,' Sokolov begins. 'Your recent visitors have discussed the security situation with Mr Bovar. It seems we have all been transferred to their employment, and they've asked that this gentleman,' Sokolov pauses, to make clear the stranger is far from gentle, 'to deliver a message.'

The blackshirt looks at Johns with menace, before bestowing a sinister smile on Polly. He produces a small, clear plastic box from his pocket and crouches down by the coffee table. He empties two ants onto the surface, between the lines of matchsticks. One of the ants is quick to recognize food and scuttles towards what are evidently grains of sugar. Just as it reaches the pile, the goon brings his thumb down hard on the remaining ant. He raises his thumb, blackened by its remains.

Johns' nervous tics fires up. 'You don't scare me.'

The smile gets wider. 'She's more use to us alive,' says the blackshirt.

Johns sees Polly's brow tighten. He senses the

physical threat of rape or torture. One of her legs begin to shake involuntarily.

'Coward,' says Johns.

His persecutor laughs.

'Professor Johns is more of a man than you'll ever be,' Polly spits with venom.

'Enough,' says Sokolov to the blackshirt with distaste. 'Get on with it.'

'Our bosses are very generous. Look, they have a gift for you both.' The goon bends to open a camera case at his feet, and reveals two wrist bands. 'Top grade kevlar. Very strong. They have GPS trackers installed. Please put out your arm; either will do.'

'This is outrageous,' says Johns.

'Not at all. You took their details, and now they're taking yours.' He moves to the side of Polly's chair and leans down to take her left arm. In one movement she sharply pivots at the waist and stands, crashing the heel of her right hand upward into the goon's face, causing him to stagger backwards, blood gushing from his nose.

Sokolov gives an involuntary cough, as though stifling laughter.

'Oh, I'm so sorry, you took me by surprise,' she says.

In the time it had taken for Johns to blink twice, she has gone from demure lab assistant to warrior, and back again.

'I did a self-defence course, Professor.' She

lowers her eyelashes, as the wounded man tries to regain composure and staunch his flow of blood with a handkerchief. He tips his head back a little, half-sits on the edge of the table near the window, and produces a wicked-looking short-bladed knife from his pocket.

'Slowly this time,' he says.

Sokolov comes forward and picks up one of the straps, together with a phial of high potency epoxy adhesive.

'I am gluing this around your wrist. It cannot be removed by anything you have here, so don't try.'

Their mission completed without further incident, Sokolov conducts his charge out of the house, leaving Johns and Polly in the dusty silence of the sitting room.

Johns opens his mouth twice, as though trying to say something.

Polly reads the distress on his face, and his doomed struggle to express any feelings. 'Let me get you some coffee, Professor.'

'I can't work for these beasts,' he says.

The house retires early that night. Two hours later, it's obvious from the sound of snoring that Johns is deeply asleep in his room. Polly is still fully clothed, and eases herself softly, in bare feet, trainers in hand, across the floorboards that groan the least. The door opens noiselessly, oiled by her the first night that they arrived. She descends with only the tiniest of sounds; just the dry wood of an old staircase creaking softly in the night.

She notes the silence peculiar to a house with no electricity. She goes to the kitchen, and gently tears off a generous strip of kitchen foil with the merest whisper of leaves rustling. Polly folds it twice, and wraps it firmly around the GPS tracker on her wrist. Moving to the front door, across threadbare rugs that cover cool slate slabs, she slips out of the cottage into the shade of the porch. The door, too, carefully lubricated on the first night. Bright moonlight floods the turning circle ... *The first few metres across the exposed gravel are the most dangerous.* She waits, listening: just the sound of a moth fluttering around her, the trickle of the stream outside and, beyond, the hushed movement of the sea over shingle, at the bottom of the valley. Her destination. Still, she waits. *Is that the sound of a footstep on gravel?* There are no shadows in motion, but even now in the deep of the night, a slight sighing breeze carries the scent of the sea and grasses up the valley.

Polly hears the sound of her own blood pounding in her ears. She breathes deeply, in-out, in-out, until her pulse drops.

It's time to go. A brief look around the edge of the porch – *All clear* – and she picks her way nimbly across the grit and beaten earth of the driveway, over the narrow strip of damp grass, and into the cover beyond: stunted trees, yellow gorse and brush. *Shoes on*, then stepping down the course of the stream. Halfway to the coast the scrub is gone, but the cutting is deep and provides shelter from spying eyes. She moves slowly, surely, ears and eyes straining for any signs of tripwires or movements. The moon is so bright, it feels like full daylight. Now she can see and hear and smell the waves moving insistently below on the fine, black, shining shingle.

At last, she has one bar of signal on her phone. She sends the full address to Xenia, together with a single word. *Help*.

33

DISCOVERY

Loge has spent a very pleasant afternoon reading in the pretty garden of his bed-and-breakfast. Now, in the height of summer, it's full of the scent of rose and lavender. The landlady is Mrs Moore, who happens to reveal that her husband died three years ago, and '… keeping the garden had been his delight'. She's a round, smiling woman, accustomed to making her guests happy. As this demands continuous activity from her, across many domains, she has a habit of wiping her hands downwards to smooth her ever-present apron. It signals the end of one task and the beginning of the next.

Loge has paid two weeks in advance and receives special treatment; he is quick to recognize that she takes particular pleasure in his company. The excellent buffet of cereals and juices and the English breakfast of eggs, bacon, mushrooms, toast and marmalade, is supplemented by the enduring warmth of Mrs Moore's smile.

On the rare occasions when no other guests are present in the breakfast room, Mrs Moore lingers both to pour tea and make light conversation. On more than one occasion, she mentions that it's lonely running the bed and breakfast on her own, before smoothing down her apron, and bustling off to the kitchen.

Loge considers contacting his son about Polly. Victor and he are almost estranged, so communication between them is tentative at best. There's no hope of his son answering an email about an ex-girlfriend without taking offence of some kind. Similarly, he thinks of discussing the matter with his wife, Valerie. That too would fail: if, after delaying to call her, he dared mention another woman, it will not be well received.

Notwithstanding the marked attention of his landlady, Loge is able to make reasonable progress in his work. Despite the poor-quality broadband, he keeps in touch with his office, oversees the technical switchover of diamond production, monitors the test-surfacing for military development and, when time allows, reviews Domino itself.

Although he's no expert – he considers coding the language of another generation – he knows enough to recognize Johns' work as elegant and economic. However, he's discovered an anomaly. It's clear to Loge that a vestigial strand exists, embedded deep within the programme. He's referred it to young Drozdov in the science department, and asked him to analyse this peculiarity; so far, he's heard nothing back.

As the day progresses, punctuated only by a pleasant salad lunch in the company of the effusive and ever-busy Mrs Moore, he discovers the mysterious link to the FTSE index. This doesn't trouble Loge particularly, but he's curious, as the scheme of the coding is otherwise so precise and accurate.

At 4 p.m. exactly, Drozdov calls. Loge notes that it must be six in Moscow, and feels a small glow of comfort knowing that his young protégé is as diligent as ever.

'What are your conclusions?' he asks, in a firm, avuncular tone.

Drozdov's thin, pale face leans anxiously in towards his camera. 'Sir, it's premature to give you an accurate answer. One thing is certain: the operation of the secondary programme is expressly not for the purpose of manufacturing diamond layers.'

'I deduced the same. It's good we are able to confirm one another's findings. Please persist with the analysis and keep me notified.'

'Sir, should we tell the president?' asked Drozdov, referring to Bovar. There was a note of trepidation in his voice; Maxim Bovar's temper was the stuff of legend.

Loge smiles to himself. 'That's unwise until we can give definitive advice.' He pauses to consider his next words. It's imperative that Drozdov understands him unequivocally, yet the instruction must remain ambiguous, to protect them both. 'We must be exact in our work. We deal in facts, not surmise. Please continue to gather evidence, and we will then submit our hypothesis to Mr Bovar. Of course, I take full responsibility for this decision.'

Despite no apparent audible or visual sign from Drozdov, Loge can sense the younger man's relief. The call ends with a decision to review matters in forty-eight hours.

Loge then sends an advice to Johns' security detail, saying that he'll visit in person tomorrow, Saturday, to discuss technical issues. *Perhaps*, he thinks, *it will induce him to reveal more about Domino than he has to date.*

34

TO CORNWALL

In the days since the visit from Finch and Kapoor, a febrile atmosphere pervades the farmhouse. The hot weather resumed, affecting the days and the nights. If the red-brick homestead wasn't such a thick-walled, solid, cool, old friend, the summer's humidity would be oppressive.

Xenia has abandoned herself to furious labour in her studio, working long hours on new work for her exhibition. She emerges only to make or share meals. She is unusually quiet. She doesn't mention Polly. Albie is immersed in the physical demands of his beloved farm: filling silage clamps. Perhaps it's hardest for Saul. A call to the paper had not gone well, and Natalie Curzon-Watson impressed on him the necessity of staying away to 'recover for at least another week'. With regard to the USB, Michael had done his best: 'I could really only guess ... it really isn't my area.' Ultimately, he advised Saul to pass it on to a mutual friend who'd be able to comprehensively decipher the code. Saul is only too aware of the sensitivity of the data and demurs.

His exploration of the rest of the material taken from Johns' office has resulted in dead ends. While MI6's investigation has piqued his interest, he's unable to make any meaningful headway. To distract himself, he lavishes love and attention on his motorbike. When he can do no more to clean, polish and tweak it, and when Albie has no use for him on the farm, he goes to have a haircut in Salisbury.

If Saul has a weakness, it's vanity. In particular he likes his hair to be just so, and a motorbike helmet does nothing to help this. When he experimented with a short crop, his wife – *Ex-wife* – said it made him look like a convict. He hasn't been able to extinguish that image. Haircuts have therefore become a bi-weekly ritual which he uses to clear his mind and settle himself. Visiting a new barber is not a problem, they just have to follow the pattern. It's cheap therapy.

Saul wakes unusually early on Saturday. He takes his laptop down to the kitchen and makes tea. As he's had some time away from the paper, he decides to review his source notes for something to compel Natalie to side with him. Then he finds it. It was there all the time, from his earliest investigation of Bovar Industries. An organigram showing the positions of key executives. *Technical Director, Loge.*

He feels his pulse quicken There's nothing about Loge's work online, but that's no surprise. In his long search for evidence, Bovar Industries seem to have done a good job of scrubbing the internet clean of anything they don't want the public to know. A search for 'Bovar Industries diamonds' reveals mass production of 'industrial quality stones.' His mouth goes dry. Saul knows his body is telling him that he's on the right track. He's already convinced that Bovar is the puppet-master behind the mining of naval vessels, and that he used someone else's security forces. *He's too clever to use his own. The question is, whose?*

Saul goes back to his list of possible Russian characters who have private military companies. As before, no names stand out. *So, Loge works for Bovar, who I know is a bad actor. He's already into making diamonds, and now we know Loge and Bovar are linked ...*

Footsteps approach the kitchen and Albie enters, frowning. 'Zee's heard from Polly. We've got the address. It sounds like she's in trouble.'

Xenia arrives, tracks of tears down her face. 'Polly's in danger.' She begins choking with sobs, and Saul hears 'Cornwall'. He feels his palms itching, as his body readies itself for a long bike trip west. When

Xenia regains composure, with Albie's arm around her and a mug of tea in hand, she shows them the pin drop: a remote location on the north-east coast. Aside from the track to the house, there are two routes nearby which look like they might offer access on foot for a cautious approach.

'Can you go?' Xenia asks Saul.

'Of course.'

'We'll follow you down there as soon as possible,' says Albie. 'There are a few things I have to straighten out here.'

'When?' asks Xenia, looking at Saul.

'The bike has a full tank, everything's ready. It'll take me a few minutes to pack, and I need to fill my water bottle.'

Ten minutes later, Albie is leaning against the upright of the barn door, as Saul climbs into his leather over-trousers.

'I didn't want to mention it in front of Xenia, but it could be dangerous. I don't have a weapon other than a shotgun, and you don't want to take that.'

'I'm not looking for trouble,' says Saul, knowing full well the visit is not likely to be social.

'No, but be prepared.'

At that moment Xenia arrives with a flask and sandwiches.

'Thanks, Saul. This means a lot to me.'

'No worries, Zee.' He swings his leg over the seat and starts the bike. 'You've told Six?'

Xenia nods. 'Won't you be too hot in your leathers?' she asks.

'Better safe than sorry. It's a four-hour trip. I'll call when I get there.'

'Be careful,' says Albie, and winks.

Saul winks back, puts on his helmet, and gently lets the clutch out on the BMW. A ball of excitement vibrates in his stomach as he looks forward to the journey, with the promise of seeing Polly at the end of it.

He raises his left hand in a wave as the powerful machine rolls heavily forward and down the dirt track, away from the homestead.

It's half an hour before Saul realizes that the trip is going to be a lot tougher than anticipated. It's the hottest day of the year, he's sure of it. The first sign is sweat trickling down his back and under his arms. He considers stopping but doesn't have alternative gear with him; all he's packed is a change of clothes and wash kit.

It's his habit to stop every two hours, no matter how a trip is going. As soon as the bike is on its stand at a service station, he drains his entire water bottle. He then strips off his leathers and carries them into the busy atrium to luxuriate in the cool of the AC.

He heads to the washroom, splashes water on his face, and refills his water bottle. He had intended to take ten minutes out under a tree to relax, but the smell of greasy chips wafting from a fast-food joint drives him back into the saddle. Revived and relieved to be back on the road, he rejoins the highway,

The total journey time is four hours, which takes him to the nearby military base, marked clearly on the map. The countryside on either side is cleft by small valleys with steep, wooded slopes. Reaching one of the access roads near the house proves to be difficult; *These little country lanes are never straightforward,* he thinks, and turns left towards the nearest village.

He contemplates parking opposite the church, in a charming little hamlet about two miles on from his destination, thinking it'll be entirely anonymous and safe if there is any difficulty. He stops, then reconsiders, wanting to get as close to the location as possible for a recce.

A short way on, the road degrades rapidly into a pitted, dried mud track, and then comes to an abrupt end in a sandy halt. *This is it.* Nearly one thirty, with the sun suspended in the mid-point of the heavens, shining in all its brilliance. Cutting the engine, all is suddenly silent and still. He takes a moment to reframe and gather himself from the trip. The stop reminds him of his visit to Ben Seiter; knowing he's close, but not knowing exactly where he is. Isolated, and unseen by the world.

He leans the bike on its side rest – it seems stable – and dismounts before gratefully peeling off his sodden leathers. The interior of his helmet is as damp as the rest of his gear. *How much weight have I lost on the trip from perspiration?* It takes almost his entire water bottle to slake his thirst. There's a cupful left, so he drinks that too. *I've still got Zee's flask if I'm thirsty.* Saul runs his bike chain through an arm and a leg of the leathers, then locks them to the bike together with his helmet. *No one's likely to pinch my stuff in this remote place, but it doesn't hurt to be careful. A born city type,* he thinks ruefully, as he pockets his keys.

He takes a moment to survey the scene around him. He can smell and hear the sea, but the coast path is invisible from here, shielded by a rise in the ground, and thick bushes of gorse, with dazzling yellow flowers. On one side, the lush green of thick uncut grasses sweeps gently uphill, in the direction of the village. On the other is a short, dusty walk across the rutted track before the drop-off to the valley and the house beyond. *Containing Polly.* The air is filled with the breath of summer and grass and hope. *I'm here to rescue the fair damsel from the dragon.*

Feeling more comfortable, he rummages in the panniers for his black baseball cap and a bandana to protect his neck. Even without the sun slowly roasting him in his leathers and the heat of the bike engine beneath him, he's still uncomfortably hot. He stows the keys in his pocket and checks the map on his phone to confirm his position: *A little over a mile to the house.* He takes a breath and starts walking. Within a minute he's reached the side of the valley. The cottage is at the top left end and clearly visible, resting just below the hill-line. He hoists Albie's binoculars which Xenia insisted he take, and examines the exterior as best he can. Nothing moving, just a pleasant cottage bathed in bright sunlight. The course of the stream, part-covered with windblown bushes and salt-stunted trees, looks like it offers plenty of protection. *What could be more innocent than a walker going for a stroll?*

The recce complete, Saul decides to let Albie know that he's arrived. He strolls back to the bike but there's no signal, so he walks a short distance across the meadow to the coast path. He's now at the top of a high cliff, his back to the valley and the cottage, looking out to sea. The rocks below are black and sharp, against which even the gentlest waves dash dramatically. The conversation is brief, but Xenia's audibly relieved to know the house truly exists and that Saul is close by.

He returns to the ridge, where another large gorse bush provides him with an excellent hide from which to scrutinize the house. He kneels down on the hard-baked earth and brings the glasses to his eyes. The first thing he registers is a flash of sunlight reflecting back from a pair of binoculars in the hands of a distant black-clad figure. *Is that a walkie-talkie in his hand?* Moments later, there's the sound of a movement behind him. It's the last thing he remembers.

35

SLEEPERS

MAXIM BOVAR ADMINISTERS the daily misting to his rare and beautiful orchids. Of the several critically endangered species, he feels particular pride in the Sang's Paphiopedilum, whose native habitat is a mere eight square kilometres of Sulawesi. He tenderly covers them. Anyone close would have heard the gentle murmur of 'Goodnight, my darlings'. *These exquisite plants thrive on almost nothing*. He admires that greatly.

He had needed time to himself. Just before the ritual of watering, he'd examined, with mounting concern, a shortfall in several of his accounts. Funds have mysteriously disappeared; millions of roubles of which he'd previously been certain. Bovar's suspicion lies squarely on a particular member of staff, so he asks secretary Chernoff to get his personal accountant on the phone.

Returning to his desk, he settles himself for the final meeting of the day; a progress report from his science team. He is tired and has enough self-awareness to allow – particularly in the light of the error in his accounts – that he may lose his temper. *Why am I surrounded by fools?*

At precisely three, there's a knock on his door and secretary Chernoff ushers four nervous-looking academic types into the room. Drozdov is among them.

'Gentlemen, your report.' Bovar's face remains impassive behind his heavy glasses. He finds that holding this expression has the required effect on visitors while they're surrounded by the splendour and size of his office. The three men and one woman stand nervously before him.

Ilyin is second-in-command to Loge, and therefore the most senior of the group. He's never presented directly to Bovar, and was therefore unaware his leader keeps his office at the optimum ambience for plants rather than humans. Twenty-seven degrees Celsius and humid. Although Ilyin wears his supreme intellectual strength lightly, he hides his social unease beneath layers of clothing. Today, this took the form of a tweed suit, waistcoat, white shirt and tie that prove too hot and too tight for these conditions. He reveres precision in all matters, yet feels confounded by the complexity of breathing, standing completely still and reporting to his employer. 'Sir, it is very early days in respect of the diamond surfacing for military innovation. We are examining the potential for adhesive surfaces, weapons' hardening and body armour. Application of the Domino programme in this respect is currently limited to small-scale experimentation. We hope to have some results of interest to you in eight weeks.'

Bovar leaves a long pause. He stares hard at Ilyin and says simply, 'Three weeks.' He nods for the group to continue.

Loge has specifically appointed Drozdov to report on diamond production. 'Sir, we have outstanding progress with Domino. Our four facilities all report a threefold increase in output of small stones. This comes, significantly, when the market price of diamonds is increasing rapidly. It appears – and I say 'appears', because we don't understand their reasoning – White Diamonds are choking supply. Our timing is fortunate.'

Bovar allows a broad smile to rest on his features, only to eliminate it almost immediately.

'Can we expect further increases in production?' he asks.

'It's reasonable to expect an incremental increase in the short term. Director Loge is aware of a technical issue, but this is, we hope, insignificant. In short, we should achieve a further ten per cent increased output in the midterm.'

If Bovar is delighted he doesn't show it and merely gives a perfunctory nod.

'I have a new proposition. I want you to examine the potential for the surfacing of non-diamond gems with excellent clarity and white colour. That is to say stones that possess similar qualities to a diamond.'

There is a brief conference between the science team, then Ilyin speaks.

'You would like us to establish the viability of coating stones that look and behave like diamonds, but are in fact not diamonds. Is that correct?'

'Just so.'

'This is in conflict with our military research. Which is the priority?'

'Both.' Bovar bestows the full, fierce fire of the rage building in him, on his glare at Ilyin. 'I want it and I'll have it. Do not return here without a good result. That is all I ask.' He waves the group away with the back of his hand, as though dismissing an irritant fly.

Bovar waits for the door to close. He draws himself to his feet, which indicates how excited he is at the spectacular development in diamond production. It promises astonishing returns, and he isn't going to sacrifice them to Bychkov and Vasiliev. Pressing the button on his intercom, he asks secretary Chernoff to fetch his head of security. Twenty minutes later, Kalov is sitting before him.

'It concerns our friends in the UK, Ivan,' he begins slowly.

Bovar knows that Kalov will be unsettled by the use of his first name. It can mean only one of two things. Getting fired or doing something that will bring his boss immense personal pleasure. The two are not mutually incompatible.

'The time has come for us to separate our interests.' He looks meaningfully into the dead eyes of his security chief.

Despite the ambiguity of the statement, Kalov nods sagely, as though he had come to the same conclusion.

'Please ensure that our friends in the UK media, parliament and other ministries understand that Messrs Bychkov and Vasiliev are guilty of heinous crimes. These include mine attacks on naval vessels around the world, espionage, and other violent activities. It is absolutely essential they are entirely disabled, and unable to pursue their business interests in Russia. While this is urgent, please execute it with all discretion. Do you require further directions?'

Kalov gives the minutest shake of the head.

'The second issue is related,' continues Bovar. 'As soon as Bychkov and Vasiliev are exposed, they will almost certainly cancel the protection of Professor Johns. He is now an obstacle. Please ensure Johns, together with anyone working with him, is eliminated. I want no loose ends. I want nothing subtle. I want everything destroyed. Is that clear? This must not get back to me; use someone at arm's length.'

Kalov nods and makes his way stiffly from the room with as much dignity as his position allows. His collar is wet with perspiration.

Relieved by this delegation, Maxim Bovar draws a few items towards him that he wishes to take to the *dacha*; his phone, his desk diary and a pair of Japanese bonsai pruning shears in their pale leather case, embossed with his initials. He carries them with him at all times.

36

BAIT

Finch and Kapoor sit on hard chairs at a cold table, surrounded by computers set up for them just hours before. They've been given refuge in an unprepossessing Nissen hut tucked away at the far end of the military base. The room is barely warmed by sunlight that streams through the white-painted steel windows. The air in here smells of old cigarettes and urine. Yet, and it pleases them both, the digital plumbing boasts even better connectivity than they enjoyed in the Hub. Human comforts are scarce here, but their job is nonetheless made easier by the virtual and physical proximity to the target site. They feel close to the action.

Zooming in from their eye in the sky, Kapoor runs the difference checker between frames from yesterday and today. He can make out the dropped motorbike as a distinct new object. Not so clear is the figure beneath. Back in London, Kapoor was able to render 3D maps of the area from the satellite images. He easily identifies the exact location of the accident. It's at the end of the track that extends from the village, above and beyond the brow of the valley hillside. He loves this Earth intelligence stuff.

'Well?' asks Kapoor, showing the pictures to Finch. 'Do we move in? It's out of sight of the cottage.'

Finch looks balefully at her colleague over the top of her spectacles. 'This looks like a set-up. He's bait.'

'How do you mean? There's a man down. The bird hasn't picked up any extra movement around Johns in the past twelve hours. We think the security hoods are static. We've got them in a sack.'

'We've got Johns, yes, but we've always had him. If, as we think, he's defected and is selling secrets to the Russians, I want all the bad guys. With him there, we may still catch them. We've got to assume the stooges are all around – we know there have been reinforcements – and we definitely don't want a gunfight.'

'So we throw a cordon round the site?'

'And show them we know? What about Loge? He's our link to Bovar. We need to pick him up at the same time as Johns.'

'The military base could run an exercise: make it

look like a normal event and then they can help the victim.'

Finch thinks for a moment. 'Let's do it, and perhaps our team can do close reconnaissance on the ground tonight. Hopefully, if it's not a decoy, they can help the man down without attracting attention.'

Her phone rings. A small voice at the other end passes on an 'advisory'. She clenches her jaw. 'I understand.' The call ends. 'We've got to go back.'

'No.' Kapoor's brow darkens.

'The balloon has gone up over Bychkov and Vasiliev. We're pulling them in. It comes from the top.' She has mixed feelings. *Might we be able to establish the link with Bovar, or is this as far as the mission is going to go?*

'We've been here before, haven't we?' she says.

'We surely have.'

Finch can see the disappointment in Kapoor. *I won't miss the stench of this Nissan hut, but we both want to be present as the net closes on Johns and Loge.*

'The longer we hold Vasiliev and Bychkov,' she reminds him, 'the more confident they'll become. We need to scare them witless before their lawyers move in.'

News of their imminent departure has a different effect on Dutton, the camp commander. He seems relieved, and immediately orders the base helicopter to be made ready for a trip to London.

'As I understand it,' he begins, 'The mission is to apprehend this character Loge, together with Dmitri Johns and his assistant, Polly Smith?'

Finch nods.

'I'm mobilizing two specialist patrols to throw a discreet cordon around Johns' cottage. They'll monitor the position from either side of the valley. We'll allow coast path walkers unless the situation escalates. The squads will be under strict instructions to avoid confrontation.'

'We don't want anyone to sense the noose tightening around them,' agrees Finch.

'Just so.' Dutton confirms, 'We won't attempt treatment of the body under the motorbike until after dark; even then, to make the minimum necessary intervention, is that correct?'

Again, Finch nods.

'We'll have an air ambulance on standby.' He pauses; *If the life of the man or woman under the bike is in imminent danger, I'll have a difficult call to make. But it will be my decision, not theirs.* 'Similarly, we won't launch a retrieval of Johns and Smith. An attempt to approach while armed guards are present will inevitably result in a pitched gun battle.'

Julia Finch winces. 'No one wants that.'

'I'll deploy uniformed soldiers on the road to keep third parties away from the site, and allow only known suspects access to the cottage. Members of the security detail around Johns are easily recognizable, and any visitors to the cottage are to be waved through. Once in, we won't let them out.'

Julia Finch stands and shakes his hand, as they hear the stutter and rush of the helicopter starting up. Kapoor leaps to his feet. 'Thank you, Commander. You'll keep us informed?'

'Of course. Every patrol member has a wearable device that sends out a continuous electronic marker, so Control can keep tabs on them. You'll have the same feed; you can see who is moving, and where they are, in real-time.'

Kapoor nods vigorously, but Julia Finch is already opening the office door.

'The tech depends on a mobile signal, which is absent from much of the target area,' he continues. 'In the past, the red dots representing the patrols appeared and disappeared on our monitors, like a demented video game. In anticipation of this exercise, I've ordered a temporary mobile mast. They're plumbing it into our main communications trunk as we speak.'

37

BURDEN

THE BASTARDS MUST HAVE DRESSED me in my leathers, then lowered the bike onto me, to cook in the heat. Shit. They've made it look like an accident.

Perversely, Saul feels humiliated.

He becomes aware of the outline of his phone on the periphery of his vision; one shiny edge just visible, and tantalizingly close to the right of his head. His left bicep is tightly trapped, but he can move his right arm. He wriggles it haltingly outwards, scraping along the hard mud and stones, stopping every few seconds to rest. At last, he releases it from the wreckage. Compared with his left limb, it feels remarkably unharmed, but the rest of him groans in disagreement. The more he twists and stretches above him to the right, the greater the complaint from the other side of his body. With two fingers – his thumb is too swollen to use – he draws the phone painfully towards him. He can't see the screen, but feels for its comforting gloss within the silicon case. Shattered. He moves his fingers, trying to ring the last number: the farmhouse.

No ring. No distant sound of Albie or Xenia's voice saying, 'Saul, Saul?' Nothing.

He forces himself to relax. *OK, that doesn't work, what might?* Emerging from a fog of thought, he remembers the sequence for an emergency SOS. *Press the On button five times, then Call.* He's unsure he's got it right ... he's unsure about everything. *Calm down. The emergency services will triangulate and find me soon.*

He fails to remember that where he lies, roasting in the sun, and out of view of the coast path, there's no signal. Nor is there a glimmer of life in his phone.

His injuries are too much of a burden, and Saul loses consciousness.

For the next twenty minutes he wavers between blackout and dim awareness. As he comes round, a single command arises like a small whispered voice urging him to wake. The more Saul wills it, the deeper he is pulled downwards to become part of a vast, overwhelming amorphous mass of heaviness. Then he feels himself float free and hover weightless above the scene. Looking down, he sees his twisted body, trapped and feeble in the glare of full sunlight. One part of him says 'Let go' while the other simply drifts suspended. Observing.

38

DRAINED

URI BYCHKOV SITS at his Louis XV walnut writing table in the library of his Richmond home, stunned by the news. Before him, his laptop is open at an email from a Swiss bank, suggesting he place his account in funds. *With our most sincere apologies, no further withdrawals may be made until such time ...'*

It had happened so fast. Just twenty-four hours before, he'd been discussing designs for a super-yacht with an established broker. Today, drained: the accounts empty. Of course, he has his mansions and his toys – for now – but they all cost money. His wits, the stash of gold in the safe and his family name are all that stand between Bychkov and destitution.

He has always been rich. His father had been rich, his grandfather had been rich, and his great-grandfather. That was the way of things for the Bychkov family. He had obtained and kept the divine right of money-power from birth. The family name hadn't played so well in the English private schools, where he developed his precocious talent for manipulation, but that was long in the past. Wealth brought honour without the tiresome requirement of integrity or service. Merely seeming to own the factories had been enough.

At end of Soviet Russia, Uri had been in his thirties and with a young family. Whilst he had managed the family firm – groomed for it from an early age – his own father swept up precious franchises in a furious buying spree. They became a conglomerate overnight, and started stripping the weak of their assets. His father died suddenly of a heart attack, passing everything to his only son.

Bychkov admits the bastard Vasiliev is more like his father, a buccaneer, but that doesn't excuse him stealing an empire. The Bychkov empire. *It is so stressful running factories. They always need capital; always problems, problems, problems. No one understands this. Especially communists.*

What will happen if I lose my wealth? Surely that's impossible ? But my own eyes don't deceive me. Huge amounts of cash are disappearing from all my accounts as a result of currency and stock trades I've never instigated. Have I lost my mind? Never!

Then another thought occurs to Bychkov: *What if it isn't Vasiliev? We both live in England, our wives are friends – or at least civil to one another – and we have children at the same school. Could that cur Bovar have set this up by from the beginning? It is he who persuaded both me and Vasiliev to work on credit, he who has the diamond interests, and he who boasts such closeness to the President of Russia. It's no secret there's a drive to 'expand and modernise the country' in all its bloated immensity. The State, in common with every government everywhere publicly declaims, 'the economy must grow,' ... and Bovar Industries has fingers in everything. Bovar can be trusted only to do what's right for Bovar, whereas Vasiliev discussed the diamond cover-up openly with me.*

Bychkov knows, in his gut, he is right.

He immediately sends a message to Vasily: *We have a problem. Call. The lives of our families are under threat.*

He picks up the phone and stabs three numbers. A private military company is useful at a time like this. *What am I saying? This will never happen again.*

'Yes, sir.'

'Firstly, I need maximum security on my family and the withdrawal of all troops from non-essential duties. Including Cornwall. Immediately. Secondly, I require a high-performance squad to conduct an operation in the vicinity of Moscow.'

'Of course, sir.'

'I require the neutralization of Maxim Bovar.'

There's an audible intake of breath.

'You will be aware of the very high security surrounding the target. This is an exceptionally demanding task, sir. '

'He'll be in his office, at home or his dacha. Are you able to mobilize for immediate action?'

'It will incur significant cost.'

'The cost is immaterial.'

'I understand, sir. Please give me the details.'

Bychkov had been a guest at Bovar's private dacha only four months prior. He dictates the address in the rural idyll of Peredelkino, outside Moscow, as well as vulnerable points of entry.

'Is there anything else, sir?'

'Expedite this immediately. Use a team whose loyalty is absolute and unquestioning. Each member, and I include you in this, will receive a bonus equal to half their salary for completing a successful mission.'

'Thank you, sir.'

There's a knock on the door. His secretary.

'Yes?' Everything irritates him now.

'Some people to see you, sir. They won't give their names.'

'Why bother me with this?'

'They say they're with MI6.'

'I'll come out.' Without missing a beat, Bychkov touches 'Legal' on his phone, and within seconds is talking to his solicitor. 'It's a code red. MI6 is here. Check Vasiliev.'

They drew straws, or more accurately, strips of paper. Finch got Bychkov and Kapoor got Vasiliev. They agreed on a list of questions for the interviews, and that they would take each man to separate secure facilities. They even synchronized their watches to ensure that they make the seizures exactly in parallel.

It came to nothing.

Having held their guests for all of one hundred and twenty minutes, the solicitors arrive. Each make it plain that, without charges, their clients must be released within twenty-four hours. They insist that, 'The accusations of our client's involvement in the campaign of mining vessels are baseless. Material evidence suggesting that my client is any way connected to these events is non-existent.' They eventually agree to house arrest for the rest of the day, and no further publicity.

To Finch, her one small satisfaction is the fact that there were plenty of newspapers happy to photograph Bychkov and Vasiliev as they arrived at the cells. *The whole thing reeks with the stink of plausible deniability,* she thinks to herself. *It's as though we've revealed an open drain in plain sight, and everyone using it denies its existence.*

As a result, a certain government minister sees fit to call her directly. He makes her position extremely uncomfortable. He clarifies that, although the UK's Terrorism Act allows up to twenty-eight days in custody, MI6 cannot invoke it without causing more friction. A lot more.

39

GONE

It's a still evening. The scent of salt water and a million summer flowers sweeps up the valley on a gentle breeze, as Polly stands outside the front door of the cottage, glass in hand. She looks out at the sparkling waves rolling towards the land far below, and turns, expecting to see the duty guard leering at her. No one. She strolls nonchalantly over to the outbuilding; now the generator is off, there's no sound. She meanders up the drive for a hundred metres, before returning to the house.

'Professor, they're gone.'

'What do you mean?'

'The goons. There's no one here.'

Johns goes out of the cottage onto the gravel and dirt apron, that serves as the turning circle. 'I believe you're right. Should we be worried?'

Polly wrinkles her nose and screws her eyes

against the low sun; it's begun its descent below the horizon of the valley, leaving another three hours before darkness. 'I'm going.'

'You can't! What will I do without you? We must continue; you know what it means if we fail ... and we won't.'

'You should leave too. We know MI6 are looking for us. Probably, the university, White Diamonds and the other sponsors as well. We need to find a safe place.'

'But our laboratory is here.'

'The work can wait, Professor. Make your mind up. I'm leaving.'

'I forbid you to go,' he says, looking directly out to sea.

Beneath the vehemence, Polly hears a near-hysterical note in his voice. She changes tack: 'Dmitri, there are dangerous people out there.' She's never used his first name before, and it has the effect she intends.

He turns to her, eye's gleaming with affection. 'Why do you say this? How foolish you are to suggest anyone will hurt us. I'll protect you.'

Polly reflects on how the human mind finds it so easy to deny the one thing that is obvious. Twenty-four hours ago, Johns had been paralysed by fear, and he still won't run to safety.

'You've met Bychkov and Vasiliev. They are not men of peace. You've seen the knives and guns of their goons and know they're capable of cruelty. Do you think any of our employers cares about us more than money? I don't believe so. Please re-consider.'

Polly turns and walks back into the cottage. The stairs ache with creaks as she climbs to the first floor. She changes and puts her washbag and a few overnight things in her backpack. Most of her clothes remain in drawers and hanging in the wardrobe. As she casts a parting glance around the room, the sweet, dry smell of thatch floods through the open window. *I need to live somewhere like this,* she thinks to herself.

Minutes later she re-emerges from the cottage, wearing a lumberjack shirt, tight jeans, and walking boots. Johns is standing in the same spot, and still looks confused.

She puts out her hand, 'Goodbye, Professor. You're sure you won't come?'

He ignores it, his jaw set in a profile of tragic determination, 'I have work to do.'

Johns doesn't turn to face her, but she can see a wet line on his cheek.

'Do you want me to take anything? A back-up drive for security?'

No answer. Polly hesitates, then leans forward to kiss him. 'I'm sorry, Dmitri,' she says, then turns to walk away. She can taste the salt water of his tears on her lips.

She leaves by the main driveway. *I have money*

and my phones. She knows where she's going and doesn't look back.

An hour later, Polly has a lift from a businessman in an SUV. The driver is a small, mousy man with tiny hands, and clings to the driving wheel as though his life depends on it. He affects a relaxed and casual tone as he confirms he's going Polly's way, and she should 'Hop in the front.' By the time she's dropped her backpack on the rear seat, he's introduced himself as Derek, and starts peppering her with questions.

'I'm sorry, may I call my friend to let her know I'm safe?' says Polly.

'Oh, of course, of course.' The flow of his chatter stops and he just grins inanely, clearly delighted at picking up such a charming passenger.

Polly is confident that her second phone is secure, and calls Xenia.

'Zee, I wanted to let you know I'm OK.'

'Polly! We've been so worried about you.'

'Didn't you get my message?

'Yes. Saul came down immediately. Are you with him?'

There's a silence as Polly digests the new information. 'He's fine. I saw him briefly, but he wants to stay on to do some research.' She pauses, balancing the need for credibility with the risk of giving the wrong information. 'Besides, he didn't have a spare helmet.' She's convinced Saul would have come by bike.

'Oh, oh great,' says Xenia. She sounds bewildered. 'I wonder why he hasn't called?'

'Maybe a flat phone battery? Can I come and stay? I need to talk.'

'Of course. Albie left for Cornwall at about six, so he should be down there soon. Can he pick you up?'

'I've already got a lift that'll take me more than halfway.' Polly pauses to smile at Derek, who beams back with pathetic gratitude. 'Can I call you when I get nearby?'

'Of course, I'll collect you, no problem.'

'Thanks Zee, I'll fill you in when I get there. 'Bye.'

Xenia is alone. At least she's stayed away, thinks Polly. Despite herself, she begins to tremble as she thinks of the danger Albie and Saul may have to face. She commands herself not to betray her feelings.

Albie had refused to take Xenia. She was furious, but deep within had accepted that someone needed to be the anchor at the farmhouse. It was the one place Saul or Polly would fly to.

Albie had expected a long journey, but it was made far worse by heavy traffic from an accident. To make matters worse, his phone had run flat and he wasn't able to call Zee from the car. He arrived in Cornwall long after dark and, as the receptionist was so keen to point out, was 'lucky to get the one available room at Bude's premier hotel'. He ordered breakfast on room service for six fifteen the next morning. As soon as he plugs his mobile in, the message arrives.

Polly's here.

He calls, but there's no answer. Any signal that allowed the text to come through is now no longer available. The landline in the room doesn't work. He goes down to reception, but they explain that all the lines are down. 'There's a problem at the exchange.' There isn't even wifi. Ever the farmer, and aware that he can't check an app, Albie strolls outside to sniff the Atlantic air. He remembers the forecast of a severe storm tonight, perhaps tomorrow. *It'll be fine*, he says to himself, goes back to his room, and falls directly to sleep.

To Finch and Kapoor, events unfolding in Cornwall seem remote from the business of making a case stick on Bychkov and Vasiliev. But at 2215, there's an abrupt change: every one of the red dots representing a member of the armed forces in the area disappears from the monitors. Their tenuous link to the operation is severed.

Calling Commander Dutton on a secure backchannel, they learn that the local engineering team, working overtime to install the mobile mast, has severed the main telecommunications cable. As ever he is professional and courteous. Nevertheless, it's crystal clear he's delighted that the spooks, over three hundred miles away, must relinquish control. They can no longer tell him how to do his job.

40

REPORTS OF THEIR ARREST

Bovar settles himself in the pleasant little conservatory adjoining the dacha. He places the freshly made cup of Turkish coffee on a small grey-blue marble table inlaid with lapis. In here, he has access to all that he loves: his plants.

When Kalov activated counter-measures to protect his boss, he explained it would require twenty armed men at the dacha. Bovar had nearly cancelled his trip to his sacrosanct country retreat, but he needed to visit his other beloved orchids. Although they live in a perfectly controlled environment, he trusts no one to care for them as well as he. *It takes a lot of money to keep me living simply,* he thinks, *but that's my business.*

Secretary Chernoff told his local staff to stay away and she arranged a replacement cook and cleaner with prior security clearance. Bovar's wife

Tatiana refused to come. *Probably just as well,* he reflects.

The house had seemed so empty when he arrived.

Kalov calls Bovar from the Moscow office at seven, to report that the security team around the dacha have taken four mercenaries captive. 'We are now in discussions, and can reduce the guard,' Kalov reports. 'The locals may return from tomorrow if you require. We have neutralized the threat.' This is agreeable to Maxim Bovar, who makes a mental note to reward Kalov on his return.

He opens his laptop to the UK online edition of the *Financial Times,* which has a feature on the background of two previously fêted members of civil society. Allegedly, they've funded a series of appalling quasi-military operations to induce fear in the world's navies. These attacks deliberately exposed the vulnerability of all ships to mines.

Bovar congratulates himself on the free advertising. *It's been a really excellent morning.*

The paper is strong on the background of the two men, but weak on facts supporting the allegations against them. It quotes the legal counsel, for both Bychkov and Vasiliev, as threatening action to sue for slander. 'Why attack such fine, upstanding supporters of UK plc?' they reason, 'What prima facie evidence is there?' Further, unattributed supporters, point out that these men have '...

generously endowed museums and galleries with buildings.' It's a veritable chorus of angels.

The article concludes that, in the absence of firm evidence, both Bychkov and Vasiliev are extremely unlikely to face charges. Indeed, as their legal representatives stress, if the hearings are inconclusive, both men will be due substantial compensation.

Bovar scoffs. All he needs to know is that the UK government has asked Russia to seize the men's assets. In this instance, the President's office has already intervened, promising total co-operation, including a statement: 'With immediate effect, we have cancelled the recent letter agreement, concerning Bovar Industries' transfer of four factories to the guilty men.' A UK government minister no less – the Right Honourable Conrad Harris MP – heralded this as 'a glowing example of Britain's excellent relationship with the Russian leadership'. The only cost to Maxim Bovar had been a splendid diamond necklace for the wife of a senior Russian politician.

From that moment all traces of Bychkov and Vasiliev – including any correspondence, call logs, contracts and rights as board members – are excised from the records of the diamond manufacturers in Russia. Bovar's version of Domino, together with his identity, has already replaced that of Bychkov and Vasiliev. All revenue will now flow directly to him.

He's heard that the daily revenue increase is substantial, so he is about to inspect the positive impact on his downstream accounts.

Logging in, he opens the summary page and is sickened by fear.

Most of the accounts show a much lower balance than he expects. His hands began to perspire. Thinking the cause must be the excess humidity in the conservatory, he levers his bulk out of the chair to inspect the hygrometer ... exactly what he would expect.

Returning to his laptop after this exertion, he sees an email from his personal accountant. As he reads, the remaining colour drains from his leathery cheeks, and sweat breaks out on his wide forehead. Analysis shows that Bovar's losses are caused by massive exposure to a large number of junk bonds and stocks that have been 'significantly discounted'. He grabs the bonsai shears and stabs the table with such force they buckle, cutting his hand deeply. A river of scarlet streams quickly across the table top. He stares for a moment in disbelief, then staunches the flow by holding his wrist to his chest. He pushes back the white wrought iron chair and staggers into the house. As he goes, Bovar's blood drips copiously onto the pristine imported white Carrara marble floor tiles.

41

DEHYDRATION

Even before night falls, Saul senses life draining from him. The long ride, the burning heat of the day, his confinement within his motorcycle leathers, his injuries and the compression on his frame have conspired to squeeze every drop of moisture from him.

A tortured sleep comes in fits and starts. Every time he wakes, it's to an orchestra of pain from the piercing sharpness of cuts and bruises. Each part of his body takes their turn to persecute him. In particular, his kidneys, his left shoulder and the agony of his throat. He tries to stay in that part of consciousness which floats in a separate dimension from the traumas.

The combination of dehydration and exhaustion lead to further hallucinations. These too are intermittent. He hears sounds, voices, footsteps.

They are so frequent, and the pain of craning his neck or even opening his eyes so great, that he stops trying to penetrate the blackness of the night.

At one point he's certain an angel is with him, holding a cup, murmuring words of comfort. Miraculously, the image slakes his thirst as he raises his head, despite the pain, to gulp what he can. He thinks perhaps it's Polly, but knows it isn't. *I've failed her. Where is she now?*

Then comes the sound of thunder rolling far out to sea, reverberating across the ocean. The storm comes closer, and the sky begins to flash. In his advanced state of delirium, it becomes a weird and threatening light show, with the source invisible to him. Saul feels that it's a mirage. But when the drizzle starts as a distant shower sprinkling gently on the grass, then on his cheeks, he opens his eyes to see droplets telescoping towards him. He's overwhelmed with gratitude. It's as if Nature herself is pouring her heart out in compassion to all on the Earth, Saul included.

The rain then bursts into a raging downpour, the thunder bellows and roars overhead and sheet lightning dazzles him. Fat drops fall and fizz on his parched lips. He can taste the sweet water. He can smell the earth and the grass and the flowers welcoming the torrent. He has to turn his head as rivulets flood his nostrils. He feels himself trying to draw every trickle of moisture deep into his core.

Saul now understands that Chance or Fate is telling him that he may survive. He knows his enemy is no longer those who would hurt him, but his own battle within; his will to live.

The storm passes. As the birds begin their vigorous dawn chorus, he feels totally disassociated. He knows life will continue with or without him. The music of the fields and a new day has begun. Somewhere deep within, he hears his mother's voice, saying a prayer by her child's bedside.

42

LOGE AND SAUL

LOGE HAS DELIBERATELY KEPT his body clock on Russian time, and wakes two hours before any other movements within the bed and breakfast.

This morning, he receives Drozdov's report of the meeting with Bovar. All seems to be in order, though Loge can see the difficulties with regard to the rogue code. *I must talk with Johns as soon as possible.* He realizes he's frowning, and it isn't yet seven o'clock. When he goes downstairs, he lets himself out by the glass-paned back door instead of going to the breakfast room. It's rained overnight. *Petrichor*, he thinks, as he breathes in the sweet smell of soil refreshed by rain. The garden is drenched clean and the cobwebs, suspended between rose stems, carry a thousand small gems in their traces. It's warm in the patches of sunlight, and every plant shines with iridescent drops of water. The scent of flowers is light and heady; soothing him.

He leans forward to pull up a small weed that's appeared overnight in the otherwise immaculate narrow gravel path way. He carries the little plant into the breakfast room, and places it tenderly on a side plate to examine it.

Mrs Moore, on hearing that her adored guest has arrived in the dining room, bustles in with tea.

'I've brought a newspaper for you, Mr Loge.'

She seems less familiar this morning, with visible strain showing. He isn't normally one to comment on these things – no doubt his own wife would call him insensitive – but he notices.

'That's very kind, Mrs Moore. How are you this morning?'

'The headline caught my eye,' she says, nodding at the paper. 'It seems some Russian oligarchs have been up to no good. I know they're your people and everything, I mean ...'

Loge scans the article. Reading between the lines, it's clear what's happened: he knows full well the chicanery of which his employer is capable. However, as Maxim Bovar's representative in Britain, Loge feels particularly vulnerable. Despite the radio silence between him and his wife, his daughter and his son, he feels deep concern. It wouldn't be the first time that a third party, seeking retribution on Bovar, harmed a senior executive and his family.

'This is serious, Mrs Moore.'

'With all respect, Mr Loge, I thought all Russians were communists; you excepted of course, you're different. The paper says these men have hundreds of millions of pounds, yachts, houses, mistresses and so on. I mean, why does anyone need more than a million pounds? There are so many people who don't have enough. In my mind, we're here to look after each other. What's the world coming to, I ask, if some people starve while others have too much? And then they want more!'

Loge folds the paper and places it neatly on the chair beside him. He feels moved beyond words. Although Mrs Moore knows nothing of his background, she speaks just as his own grandmother had spoken to him as a child. He had grown up under the care of good people who had suffered extremes of poverty for their beliefs as Soviets. The passion which Mrs Moore invokes, resonates deeply within him.

He looks up. 'I'm ashamed of my countrymen. They do no credit to themselves or to Russia. I agree wholeheartedly with your sentiment; it is a tragedy of the world that it reveres riches and neglects simple goodness. We do need to look after each other.'

He sees Mrs Moore's kind eyes filling with water. *Perhaps I've gone too far.*

In silence, she turns and leaves. He doesn't know what he can do to protect his family. *Now, I can only write. I will tell them what they mean to me.*

Loge knows he must confront Johns about the extraneous code. Standing by the front door, he reassures himself. *I will make it like a chess game.*

His small hire car stands directly across the road, in the morning sun. It takes a few minutes to cool. The smell of the interior plastic and paint is simultaneously fresh and nauseating. Rather than leave immediately, he examines the Ordnance Survey map. When visiting Johns' cottage, he'd caught glimpses of the sea sparkling and gleaming at the end of the valley. He hasn't yet stood on a British beach or touched its chilly waters. A childlike prompt from within tells him he must find equilibrium, despite the deep and disturbing currents in his heart.

The map shows a hamlet and a narrow road near the cottage to bring him close to the coast path. He can at least take some deep breaths of sea air before the coming showdown. He sets off, calmed by the motion of moving steadily eastward, beneath a blue sky and with vibrant greens all about him.

He finds the tiny road that leads to a peaceful village drowsing in the morning sun. He slows, as the surface becomes little more than a dirt track. He sees the gleam of metal – a motorbike – and assumes it's been dumped. Loge is disappointed that someone has defiled a place of such beauty, but gets out, ready to walk up to the coast path. Then he makes sense of the debris ... *There's a body.* For a moment, he wants to retreat to the safety of his small car, reverse up the track and pretend he hasn't seen anything. *I have too much threat in his life. Too much danger, too much drama. I'm a scientist, not a soldier.*

Then he remembers his conversation with Mrs Moore, not an hour ago, '... here to look after each other.'

He walks gingerly towards the fallen rider, trying to determine whether the body is alive. The figure moves its head. The cuts and bruises on the face are almost disfiguring.

Loge stoops at the victim's side.

'Can you hear me?'

The young man's eyes plead with him; only the shadow of a croak emerges. As Loge kneels, he realizes, with a lurch in his stomach, that the boy looks exactly like his own son. He's gripped with a terrible fear. His brain knows Victor is somewhere in Russia serving with the armed forces, but this man, crucified beneath his own machinery, speaks to another part of his being.

Loge wonders whether he might be able to lift the bike. Instinctively he knows it's impossible. He's a seventy-year-old, unfit academic, who finds a long flight of stairs a challenge.

'You need water,' he says.

The broken figure gives a faint nod. Loge looks around for a vessel and sees the helmet a few metres away. He remembers the little stream running down from the cottage.

'I'll get you some, as fast as I can.'

Again, a nod that's too painful to watch.

He crosses to the brow of the valley, taking the most direct route down to the stream below. As he walks, he scrambles to tear out the lining of the helmet, oblivious to the gorse scratching him through his trousers. By the time he reaches running water he's exhausted but exhilarated. Casting his eyes up towards the cottage, set perhaps half a mile away, he wonders whether he should go on to get help.

First things first, he thinks, *the man needs fluid.*

Cradling the precious water, he climbs the long slow rise back towards where the victim lies. Loge's heart beats hard in his chest with the exertion of climbing the slope, and breathlessness forces him to stop at least four times on the ascent. By the time he regains the brow he's dizzy with exhaustion, and once again in the full glare of the morning sun.

It's hard to pour from the helmet without drowning the young man in a gush of liquid, but every drop seems to revive him. Loge keeps thinking of the image of the Virgin Mary giving succour, on a tiny icon treasured by his grandmother. In some strange way, he feels he's giving his own son life, and finds himself mouthing Victor's name with increasing fervour. He pulls himself back to the present. *I must try to free the boy.*

'Can you talk?' he asks.

'I'm Saul,' comes the shattered voice.

'Loge. It's lucky this machine didn't catch fire.' Though scientifically accurate, he realizes how crass this must sound.

'Toast,' comes the answer with the faintest of grins in the sunburnt face. 'No accident.'

'What do you mean?'

'Bad people.'

Loge had suspected, but dared not believe. 'I need to get you out of here.'

He looks about him for something to use as a lever. There are plenty of good-size rocks for a fulcrum, but nothing available for the rod. Nor did he see anything useful on the way to and from the stream.

'Saul, I'm can't move the bike, but I know where I can get help; it's close.'

Saul closes his eyes.

Loge doesn't want to leave this vulnerable young man who has already endured so much, but knows what he has to do. He gets in the car and reverses as fast as he dares, back up the road.

43

NO ENTRY

ALBIE HAS SLEPT BADLY. There is still neither mobile or landline signal. Room service deliver lukewarm coffee and stale croissant – tasting of plastic-infused cardboard – which offer neither pleasure nor nourishment. He waits for the kitchen to open for breakfast and leaves shortly after seven thirty, with the aim of driving straight to the cottage. An armed soldier stops him near the turn-off. He's bristling with an efficiency and superiority born of being at his post at least three hours before any normal citizen wakes. He curtly explains that they're on a drill, with no civilians allowed in the area. The same applies on two other access roads. Still no signal.

Albie parks in a nearby village, on a scrap of rough ground at the midpoint between a splendid sixteenth-century manor house, and an ancient lychgate to a venerable church. He remembers his mother telling him of a folk belief: the spirit of the last person buried in a churchyard stands sentinel until the next soul arrives. Here, with no sound other than a gentle breeze, it seems feasible. A friendly labrador greets him as he gets out of the car, and he considers borrowing him. It may be useful to present himself as a local dog-walker. He's good with all animals, but this one's having none of it and scampers off, clearly hoping his new friend will play catch-me-if-you-can.

Sure that he can cross to the coast path on foot, Albie swings himself over a five-bar gate and walks a few hundred metres across thick damp grass that swishes his loafers as the track rises. At the crest of the hill, he finds yellow tape across a gap between two hedges.

He's about to duck under, when another unsmiling squaddie approaches from the other side to give him a civil but firm, 'No entry here, sir.'

'My young brother's camping.'

'He'll have been asked to move on, sir. This is a military drill.'

'He's a bit simple. He'll be frightened.'

'Not to worry, sir. We're used to that. He'll be treated with all due care and respect.'

Albie retreats to the Range Rover, feeling less than charitable towards the armed forces. Although his neighbours regard him as a solid citizen, his true attitude to the Establishment is similar to Saul's: a general respect for individuals and institutions, but a healthy scepticism of hierarchies. He takes some comfort in the non-news on the radio, as he drives away from the area. His mood improves enough to enjoy the beauty of the countryside rolling past beneath a rapturous blue sky, free of any hint of further rain.

Two villages on, he finds a car park overlooking the sea and, at last, a mobile signal. He calls Xenia.

'Albie! I'm so relieved. I've been so worried. Polly's here, but there's no word from Saul. Is he with you?'

'No sign. I can't get to the cottage. The army are doing some kind of drill'

'Polly said that Saul was going to do some research. What's that about?'

'No idea. There's been no phone signal since I got down last night.'

'But you're calling me now.'

'It's just come on. How did Polly get there? What's going on?'

'It's complicated. She's pregnant and the father is being difficult. I'll tell you when I see you. There's no sign of her yet. She's normally up for her run by now ... Is it hot there?'

'Warming up.' Albie climbs down from the front seat. 'I can't find my binoculars.'

'I forgot to say, I gave them to Saul.'

'I really do have to find him. I'll call you as soon as I have news.'

Albie puts in a call to Saul's mobile, which goes straight to voicemail.

What is that girl Polly playing at? She doesn't look like the type to get emotional. Still ...

He walks briskly to the stile and clambers over, admiring the quality of pasture, and allowing himself a moment's fantasy of grazing his own dairy herd.

On reaching the coast path, he pauses to take in the glittering ribbon of sea extending far east and west, with a black line of majestic cliffs rising and falling into the distance. *I reckon it's about three miles to the cottage*, he thinks, *But there's a lot of up and down in between*. The military base is clearly visible on a distant hilltop to the west, and he looks around for more evidence of the military cordon. A short way ahead, but inland, there's a small group of figures. *That must be them,* he thinks. The coast path itself seems free of hindrance and he sets off, determined to look like a regular walker.

A few minutes later, he hears the sound of breathing close by, and turns to see a lone female jogger running towards him. Her baseball cap and blue wraparound shades obscure much of her pale face. She passes him with her long ponytail swinging to and fro' with each pace, her broad shoulders and slender limbs moving with the co-ordinated power of an athlete. She wears a long, black backpack, and her skin-tight joggers show the outline of a firm posterior. Albie grins to himself, amused by the fact that ten years before he would have – metaphorically speaking – run after anything with a heartbeat. He thinks how lucky he is to have found Xenia. By instinct, he reaches inside his jacket pocket for a cigar to celebrate this good fortune. His hand closes around the vape which he's meant to be using instead. Then, remembering his mission, he releases it and strides purposefully on. *Maybe later*, he thinks, *Disgusting habit anyway*.

44

SAVE HIM

LOGE IS TREMBLING at the wheel of his car. His body shaken by the exertion of climbing the hillside, and the delayed shock from finding Saul. Within four hundred metres of joining the main road, he's stopped by a British soldier. He keeps the car running.

'I'm sorry sir, we're conducting a military exercise and not allowing any traffic through.'

'Officer, this is a matter of life and death. There's a young man in a motorcycle accident nearby. He needs help urgently. Please go to his aid.'

The soldier scrutinizes the older man. 'Of course sir. I'll alert the police and they'll deal with it immediately.'

'You don't understand. He's desperately in need of help.'

'Of course, sir. I can't move from my post, but I'll radio it in immediately.'

He turns and walks away from the car, speaking on a handset.

Loge is sure he hears the word 'suspect' and deduces the military exercise may be an active threat, 'Officer, I live here: the first turning on the right.'

'You're a resident? I understand. Sorry to have inconvenienced you, sir.' He turns and salutes as Loge accelerates toward the cottage, convinced he can't rely on the soldier to help with Saul.

He finds Johns at work in the outbuilding, dressed in an old striped T-shirt, long blue shorts, grey socks and tan leather sandals. He looks haggard, pale and unwashed, as though he hasn't slept in twenty-four hours.

'I'm relieved to find you here,' Loge says. 'We must leave immediately. Where's Polly? There are soldiers on the road, but if we go now ...'

Johns glances up, inspects the older man's pale and worried face, and continues working. 'No. I have things to do here. Polly has gone. Everyone's gone.'

'You're in danger. Both Vasiliev and Bychkov are under house arrest. It will only be a matter of time before you have a visit. I know my employer. He's ruthless.'

Johns looks at him, astonished.

Loge continues, his breath wheezing and his chest constricting with anxiety, 'I found a young man trapped beneath his motorbike. I'm convinced the guards beat him and left him for dead. If you don't value your life, consider your work: it's too valuable to compromise. I can get you out of the country. We can travel and work out what to do next. Bovar will be fine when things calm down; our original agreement will work. Your relationship with Vasiliev and Bychkov has ended.'

'Good, they're animals.'

'I find business has no law but that of the jungle.'

'You don't understand, Loge. No one will dare touch me. I've built Domino with an insurance scheme.'

'You mean the extra code?'

'So you've discovered it. The current copies are lethal, financially speaking.'

'I think you underestimate my employer. He has huge resources. He'll use violence to ensure he gets what he wants.'

Johns blanches. 'Who's this man you rescued?'

'His name is Saul. I couldn't release him; I'm too old and weak. He needs your help.'

Johns turns back to the diamond forge. 'I have my work to complete.'

'I beg you, Johns. I would come with you, but I'm exhausted and need to rest. You can get him out using a lever. There are rocks for a fulcrum.'

Loge can see Johns is processing the information.

'What will happen if I don't?' asks Johns.

'He will die.' Loge tries to look into the soul of Johns. *Is this a good man, who cares about other people, or only himself? Is he worth saving?* In that moment, it's vitally important for Loge to know the answer.

'OK,' says Johns. He passes Loge a handwritten manual. 'Close the machines down. As soon as it's done, you can open the forge and take the samples out. Pack them in a bag – there's one in the bedroom – together with some clothes for me. Where's the accident?'

Great relief floods Loge. *All will be well.*

'Come.' Loge leads Johns out and points across the valley. 'Just over there. Close to where we verified Domino for your unwanted guests. You can walk across in the time it would take us to drive. That way, you'll miss the soldiers.'

'There are soldiers?' asks Johns, alarmed.

'Just a drill, but we can't be sure.'

Johns walks over to a panel and throws a switch. The power is cut instantly. 'Screw the shutdown. I'm going.' He bustles outside to turn the generator off, then retrieves a long iron bar from the garden shed.

As he goes toward the house, Loge follows with laboured breathing, moving slowly, and stopping for a rest.

'I need something to protect me from the sun,' says Johns.

'Sunglasses. You need sunglasses.'

'It's not so bright.'

'To evade recognition.'

'You've been watching too many spy stories.'

Whilst he goes upstairs, Loge finds a litre bottle of water in the kitchen.

The professor returns from the bedroom, wearing a floppy hat and a pair of incongruously oversize frames.

Loge, hands the bottle over. 'He needs this. Good luck.'

Johns sets off down the valley, the sun in his eyes.

Two thousand miles away, a frantic Maxim Bovar continues to contact his accountant and brokers, ordering them to freeze all foreign exchange trading in his name. Bovar trusts Loge implicitly in all matters of technology, so calls him too. No reply. He phones Kalov, 'I need Loge in Moscow. Now.'

45

RELEASE

Johns knows exactly where to go. He's passed by the track so many times, in those innocent days of a walk to the nearest village. It seems another world to him now. He hurries as best he can, to meet the winding path that tracks up the long slope. The iron bar, filling him with power and purpose before he left, causes his arms to ache with exertion. He has to leave the bottle of water, as soon as he starts up the slope. His striped T-shirt sticks to his narrow frame. His heart is beating hard, as much from anxiety, as the climb.

Nothing Loge said has prepared him for the state of Saul: unmoving, face covered in gashes of caked blood, and body trapped like a helpless fly in a web. Johns' nervous tic tugs at his cheek. Saul is unconscious and doesn't respond to Johns' prompts Panic wells; he can't think what to do. Even if he's able to lift the bike, he can't simultaneously draw an inert body to safety.

He tests for a pulse on the carotid ... Saul gives a spasm, as though in acute pain. *At least he's not dead.* The thought of a cadaver on his hands compounds his anxiety. He sees now the mortal danger that Polly and Loge spoke about; *if the military find me first, they'll think I'm a traitor ... and what happens to traitors?* He begins to shake with nerves. *I must do something. Act. Now,* he thinks.

He rolls a large nearby rock unsteadily into position and props the iron bar across it, to a purchase point under the bike. He gingerly tests the weight, aware of what a slip might mean. *It's too much.* His thoughts go to the growing heat of the day, the comatose figure of Saul, and his own puny strength in relation to the scale of the problem. An image looms up in his mind's eye of a huge sculpture seen by the roadside in London, many years ago, when still a child. Atlas was so manly, so vigorous, so powerful; naturally he'd be able to move the world. Even then, Johns had scant confidence in his physical prowess.

He runs now, as fast as he's capable towards the coast path. He stands there, hands on knees, panting. Half-raising his head, he sees the slim figure of a jogger approaching in the distance from the east. He stands, and starts waving his arms, crying for help.

The runner comes close, but doesn't reduce

speed. Johns stretches his arms out as wide as possible, showing he'll block her progress, whatever she tries to do.

'It's an emergency. I desperately need your help,' he yells.

The woman stops abruptly. Her red baseball cap shading the intensely blue, wrap-around shades, her jaw set. Then she smiles. Her perfect white teeth ... the picture of perfect health.

'This way; very close,' says Johns, greatly relieved.

He leads her round the gorse, along the flattened grass, to the track where Saul sprawls, still unconscious.

'I need you to take this lever and push down to lift the bike. Can you do this?'

He goes to Saul's head and prepares himself to haul the limp figure by the shoulders, away from the machinery. Before he has a chance to say, 'Ready' the girl lifts the bike, leaving Johns just a moment to heave with all his might. To his surprise, he drags the inert body easily across the loose dirt and stones. He sits back for a moment, eyes closed, gasping for breath, amazed by the energy he feels surging through him. He opens his eyes to thank the stranger, but she's gone.

Vanished.

. . .

Finch calls Dutton at the military base, as she has done every thirty minutes; usually without success. Now, he answers immediately. 'The latest eyes-on intel shows no guard remaining on the target. As the safety of my men is my first consideration, we'll run a thorough confirmation by sending a walking party into the zone. Within minutes, I hope.'

46

THE WALKER

Loge slumps in the tattered, chintz-covered armchair by the wood-burning stove. The musty smell of ancient fabric mixes with the soot dust that still pervades the room. A sweet top note comes from the drooping head of the wild flowers in the little vase. Strong sunlight streams through the window, warming him. *Truly, it's been an exhausting morning*. Although just seventy-one, his life has been one of either quiet repose and study, or sandwiched between endless meetings, wrapped in wreathes of heavy cigarette and cigar smoke, stuffed between impossible deadlines. The tiredness isn't just physical, but emotional; that's why he's made his decision.

He hears the soft crunch of a footfall on the gravel near the front door, and the sound of the door handle.

The outline of a tall figure stands in the doorway.

'I was expecting you. What is your name?'

'Domino.'

Loge is grimly amused by the deliberate irony.

'Where's the girl?' the figure says.

'Gone.'

Loge's thoughts fly to his wife, and then his children. He feels a final flowing out of love to them.

Then comes the bullet.

His assassin lowers her silenced pistol, and strides over to check the pulse of her victim, her ponytail falling forwards onto his face as she does so. A single shot was all it took. She begins a methodical search of the cottage, moving noiselessly from room to room, and swiftly up the stairs. It isn't until she reaches Johns' bedroom, and sees a framed photo of him receiving an award, that she realises her mistake. Her target is the man she met on the hill, not the one in the armchair.

She leaves the cottage, scouts around the outbuilding, and finds a cage containing eight cylinders of specialist gases. It's unlocked, she opens the door. Completing the circuit, she pauses at the soundproofed power unit, still warm, then enters the outbuilding. She surveys it meticulously for any sign of life hiding in the shadows, then leaves to check the little shed in the garden. Leaving the hut door open, she places an infrared beam with an alarm. She wants no surprises.

The reconnaissance complete, she re-enters the lab, unshoulders her backpack and draws out packets of C-4 explosives to position them at the forge. Moving back outside, she places more on the vents of the generator and inside the gas cage. The timers are set for fifteen minutes. Her stopwatch is running. Another infrared beam across the outbuilding door.

Re-entering the cottage, she sets further C4 inside the kitchen, oven gas on for maximum explosive effect, and sets the timer for twelve minutes. Passing back towards the living room, she that sees Loge's lifeless body has sagged down the chair. She pauses to face him. '*Prosti*. I am sorry,' she says aloud, and bows her head for a moment.

Eleven minutes remaining.

A rumbling chatter of distant helicopter blades breaks the silence.

She'd hoped to catch Johns returning home before her departure; *I must change my plan.*

She scans the hill line with binoculars ... there are no eyes on her. She crouches and moves unhesitatingly across the turning circle to a holding position in the scrub opposite the house. The helicopter is out of sight, but its beating blades reverberate in the valley below.

She calculates: *If forces are arriving, it will take at least six minutes for troops descending by foot down the hillside after they land. A vehicle approaching from the main road could be here in seconds. There's no sign of the target. Nine minutes remaining. I must go.*

Alerted by Johns' shouting from the coast path, the advance party finds both him and Saul sprawled on the ground by the motorbike. They immediately call in the air ambulance. Albie arrives soon after. On explaining he'd been looking for his brother, he's taken aside for questions.

The helicopter lands, with impeccable skill, exactly by the site. The medics stabilize Saul as best they can before airlifting him out. A squad car arrives to take Albie back to his own car. They confirm the helicopter will go to Plymouth Hospital.

It's only now that Johns identifies himself to the soldiers. He explains that he's alone and just wants to go home, so three men escort him. They haven't gone more than a few metres down the slope, when the air is rent by two tremendous explosions, seconds apart. Then a further two. Debris showers the hillsides. The pungent, sulphurous air from the ignition of the gases drifts up towards the little group. Johns' immediate instinct is to run, to save what he can, but his escorts restrain him, warning there could be more detonations. He sits heavily on the ground, as raging fire takes his house, and a heavy pall of smoke rises from the shattered remains of the outbuilding.

He begins sobbing, his head between his knees

47

FARMHOUSE

'I'M on my way to Plymouth,' says Albie. 'Saul's being flown there by helicopter for triage. Long story.'

'You're OK?' asks Xenia, the anxiety in her voice pouring across the airwaves, in an unleashed torrent of feeling, that only lovers can know.

'Perfect. The worst thing I had to do was run along the coast path a few hundred yards. I wish I could say the same for Saul. They roughed him up really badly, and trapped him under his motorbike. It was touch and go, but the doctors say he's going to be fine. He's sedated and asleep.'

'Who's they? They beat Saul up? I don't understand.'

'Nor do I. The police are with him. Something to do with MI6.'

'This is mad,' says Xenia, on the brink of tears.

'Maybe Polly can shed some light on this. He's unconscious.'

'I'll talk to her. Take good care, my darling. Call me as soon as you have some progress. Get some sleep when you can.'

Right on cue, Polly enters the kitchen.

'That was the Albie ... from the hospital,' says Xenia, still gripping the handset, her eyes like stones.

'What's happened?' Polly reaches out a hand to comfort her, but Xenia recoils.

'It's Saul, he nearly died. Apparently, he was beaten within an inch of his life, and left underneath his bike.' Xenia's mind is churning, as she tries to make sense out of the madness. 'What's happening, Polly? We've had MI6 here, asking about Johns. What's the connection between the two of you? This is desperately serious.'

'I'm as confused as you are, Zee. Johns is my boss, and I do as I'm told. When I had the chance to work more closely with the professor, of course I took it. It seemed too good to be true.'

'Too good to be true ...' Xenia trails off into her own thoughts. 'Is there something you're not telling me, Polly?'

'I've lost the baby,' says Polly, choking the words, as though simultaneously trying to swallow the bitter truth.

'Oh God, P, I'm so sorry. This must be so difficult for you. What am I thinking?'

'It doesn't matter now. I'd rather not go there at the moment. Sorry.' Polly turns, dabbing her eyes. 'I'll be back in a minute,' she says, and leaves the kitchen.

Xenia hears her hurried steps on the stairs. The harder she tries to make sense of everything, the more the feelings of doubt and disturbance grow. She trusts her instincts, but just doesn't know what, or who, it is she doubts. It's as though the walls of the venerable farmhouse themselves are somehow unreal.

Poli Kuznetsov reaches into the side drawer and pulls out the secure mobile she's protected throughout the mission. Opening Telegram, she texts a message to her handler: *Repatriate immediately. Situation impossible. I have all elements.*

Of course, she feels bad deceiving Xenia, but that had begun years ago when they'd met at the Freshers' Fair; the first time she'd used her English pseudonym. She'd been taught to make lies as easy as possible to use, and to feel entirely natural doing so. *I was just being myself ... my new self.* The St Petersburg military academy had schooled her with skills in apparent empathy and manipulation. It had taught her to lure unsuspecting targets into total faith in her. Trained her to maintain a persona – that no one could penetrate – so they spilled their secrets to the State.

If the cost has been to draw a simple, red line, to falsify a pregnancy test, ensuring I had somewhere safe to go, that's just how it is. The only moment of genuine concern was when Victor's father recognized me. Johns had never suspected; he was too much of a fool in love.

Albie and Saul's involvement was unplanned, but it's all in a greater cause. It's my job. Russia needs Domino, and now I have both the programme, and the specialized knowledge to optimize it. I even have my contract with Bovar Industries, which may still prove useful.

Yes, she has at last fulfilled the faith put in her, when a representative of the President personally selected her from a beauty contest. That, together with her native skills and outstanding grades in the sciences, assured her extraordinary career. There are very few with such qualifications in the intelligence services. Poli feels her true and ultimate boss, the supreme head of state of the Russian Federation, will surely be well pleased. And White Diamonds, who respectfully requested the support of the State in securing Domino for their exclusive use, will also be satisfied.

I don't need to know any more. I've done my duty to my mother country. By tomorrow morning, I'll be in Moscow.

48

THIS NEVER HAPPENED

SAUL OPENS ONE EYE. The other feels like it's welded shut. A drowsy numbness seems to come and go like seaweed on the edge of a shore, caught in the restless waves ... but, at least, he can feel again. This is a mixed blessing, as his left shoulder and throat ache ferociously. *Still,* he thinks, *better that than oblivion. It's light, just after six on the clock. Morning or evening?*

He regards his brother, asleep in the green, plastic armchair, his arms folded across one another. Albie must sense Saul's single eye resting on him, and opens both of his.

'How's the bike?' asks Saul. He realizes, with amazement, that the croak of the voice is his own.

'In better shape than you are,' says Albie. 'And where are my bloody binoculars?'

Saul wants to say, 'Around the neck of some

hoodlum,' but gives up at the first syllable. He dimly remembers the agony on the hillside, and feels grateful for the small improvement. But nauseous.

'Good to have you back,' his brother says. 'I'm told I have to call the medics now, OK? Then I can have my breakfast.'

Saul gives a thumbs up with his right hand, while resting it on the bed. Even that hurts.

Within moments the doctor, together with a nurse, are by his side, running tests and scribbling onto paper charts. The doctor brings with her a brisk energy and precision, that is impossible to ignore, even to Saul in his semi-comatose state. Her youth belies her authority and confidence, and he feels in safe hands. Nevertheless, he strains to get a glimpse of the diagnosis. Illegible.

The doctor smiles. 'You're a journalist, I believe?'

He nods, weakly.

'A good one, that deals in facts. We need more of that. Keep going.' She smiled, as though the most important part of her prognosis was complete, then nodded at the nurse, who set to work. 'You're stable and making good progress; we're going to withdraw the drips. You may feel like a donkey kicked you hard in your left shoulder and throat, and we think that's pretty much what happened. You will heal. You're past the worst.' Without raising her head, her eyes turned to Saul, appraising him carefully over the top of her glasses. 'How's the pain?'

Another thumbs up, followed by a wince.

She glanced down at her notes, 'We'll give you something extra to help with that. There are some people here to see you. They're under instruction not to tire you, but we have to let them in. Do you feel ready?'

Saul and Albie exchange a look.

The nurse and doctor leave. Moments later, Julia Finch and Paresh Kapoor enter, clutching paper cups of black coffee. Both have bags under their eyes; their clothes crumpled.

'No flowers?' says Albie, 'It's lucky he doesn't need an undertaker.'

Saul does his best to let his eyes glaze over. It isn't difficult.

'We're glad to see you're recovering,' says Julia Finch, then, turning to Albie.

'It's about Polly Smith,' says Finch.

Saul can hear the words, but it doesn't make sense. *Why are they talking about Polly? Is she here?*

'What about her?' asks Albie.

'When did you last see her? Do you know where she is now?'

'With my wife, at the farmhouse. Why?'

Kapoor immediately calls the local police, asking for a response unit from a local air base to attend the farmhouse.

'We need to talk to your brother alone.' says

Finch, gesturing for Kapoor to take Albie from the room.

'Of course, I'll step outside,' Albie says, raising his eyebrows at Saul, and mouthing the name of their former prep school headmistress.

As the door closes, Julia Finch regards Saul in his bed, 'The doctor tells me you're ready for this, but sedated. Do you remember me from the farmhouse?'

Saul allows several breaths before croaking, 'Yes.'

'I'll try to keep it brief. As a journalist, it will be hard for you to hear: this never happened. Not this meeting, nor the events in Cornwall, nor the events leading to it. Am I clear?'

Once again, Saul allows himself a couple of breaths before responding. He nods his head very gently and his brain jars, even with that minute movement.

'Did you see the people that attacked you?

'No.'

'Did you see the people that rescued you?'

'No.' He feels himself drifting, detached.

'Do you know who's responsible for this?'

Saul tussles with the leaden weight of unconsciousness, bearing him down, to grasp the idea forming in his mind: *Bovar*.

Now it's the turn of Julia Finch to remain silent.

'We know you uncovered a story about the mining of ships. We know your conclusion.'

Saul takes in the words, turning them over as

though a child with building bricks, tumbling. They seem like nice words, but they won't stay still.

Finch continues, 'The good news is, thanks to you, the navies of the world, with whom we share our intelligence, also know this. The bad news is that you can't tell your story. Not yet.'

Saul closes his eyes, and allows the sedation to take him. He can't fight his own government, let alone an international business empire. He believes in the necessity and the power of journalism to tell the truth; he believes in a press that's free of control by the state, but recognizes that here is a limit which he's tried to exceed. He feels vulnerable, his muscles limp and heavy, oblivion calling him downward. He lets the story go, as though saying a last farewell to an old friend that he'll never see again.

'Saul, there's one more thing. Saul?'

He hears the woman's voice, as though far off. He doesn't want to return, he wants to sleep. He is sliding noiselessly down the sides of an endless slope, into some dark and hidden realm, remote from the living. He's safe there. Voices reverberate in the distance, barely audible.

'Saul, wake up, I have to go home.'

'Why?' says Saul. His voice is slurred.

'Zee's in danger. I've got to go, right now,' says Albie.

'I'm coming.'

'No you bloody well aren't.'

'Help.' Saul starts to swing his legs out of the bed. The room is swimming away from him, and the ground is impossibly far from his head, but as he slips forward, the touch of the cold hospital floor on his bare feet helps to rouse him.

'Clothes'

'Forget it, you need to stay here, bro.'

One look is all it takes. Although it was a close contest at the time, Saul long ago beat his brother in the game of Stubborn-O. Albie helps to ease Saul into the filthy and tattered remains of his clothing.

If Finch and Kapoor appear astonished to see the patient out of bed, the doctors and nurses are even more so. They try to dissuade him from discharging himself, but it's impossible. Accepting the inevitable, they give Saul a bagful of medications and point to a wheelchair. Albie begs a blanket, and guides the ex-patient to a lift, then on to the main entrance at maximum speed. Saul remains in the atrium, breathless from the pain of the journey from bed to doorway. Albie collects his car. Parking immediately outside the main doors, in a disabled bay, he shovels his brother across the back seat, covers him up, straps him in – ignoring the howls of pain – and sets off to the farmhouse as fast as he can.

Saul hears Albie swearing softly to himself about his brother's pig-headedness, and then a chuckle.

'Wha—?' says Saul, determined not to sleep. *I must focus. I must stay awake.*

'I was thinking of you being chased by a boar after his bucket of nuts.' Then he hears Albie check himself. He can sense his brother's anxiety about Xenia.

'Luh-nuh.'

'What's that? You OK?'

Clearer this time. 'Lon-non.'

'No Saul, we're going to the farmhouse.'

'Lon-non. Must go ... pa-er.'

'Fine, I'll drop you at the station. You can catch a train and be at the office in a couple of hours. Is that what you want?' He looks again in the rear-view mirror.

Saul is pushing himself up from the seat and glaring back. Although his voice is weak, shaken and rasping, the fierce determination is clear. 'Lonnon. Zee, the— Lon-non.'

'For fuck's sake, Saul, get a grip.' Albie glares back through the mirror to see his brother give another thumbs up.

'Than— bro.' Saul drops back onto the seat, closing his eyes.

By the time they arrive, there are three squad cars, and two armed police outside the back door. Xenia is in the kitchen, gripping a mug of herbal tea, her face streaked with tears, and deep lines of strain on her forehead and around her eyes. She bursts into tears as Albie enters, and they embrace tightly, her body shaking, speech beyond her, as he holds her for several minutes, her breathing laboured and halting.

At last, Xenia regains some composure. Tears streak her cheeks.

Albie speaks. 'Saul's in the car, and says he has to go to London to see his editor. I know ... don't ask. He's crazy, but we owe him. Will you come?'

'I'm not staying here. I'll get my things.'

The policewoman, who's been in the room the entire time, explains that they can't leave.

'Are you telling me I can't be with the one person who'll lay down his life for me? I'm going. Now.'

Natalie Curzon-Watson is leaving the office for lunch, when she receives the call.

'I'm coming in,' says Saul from the rear of the Range Rover, as it slows to join the steadily moving sea of traffic, rolling forwards, along the main artery from the west into the city.

'Have you been drinking? You sound strange. I can't see you right now. It'll be good to have you back, but only if you're ready.' The undertone of threat is unmistakable.

Saul ignores it. 'You'll want to hear this.'

'No I won't. I'm leaving for lunch. I'll see you tomorrow.'

'Natalie, in one hour. You'll know when I see you. Please.'

They'd said the blue-green capsules might perk me up a bit, thought Saul. *The first two certainly worked.*

Ella is the twenty-three-year-old receptionist at *The Inquirer*. She longs for the day that someone will recognize her writing, and invite her to work on the paper. She wants to be one of those bright, confident journalists in their bright, confident urban clothes, making up bright, confident opinion pieces. In particular, she has a soft spot for Saul, but isn't so young as to be unaware of his intellectual rigour and candour. In truth, she both adores and is terrified by him.

Today, he's unrecognizable. She's shocked and confused by his filthy and ragged clothing, bruises, stitches and unhealed wounds daubed with iodine. Albie helps him across the open-plan office, as Saul's work colleagues gape in astonishment.

'I'll do this,' says Saul, as they arrive at the door of the editor's dazzling glass, corner unit.

Natalie Curzon-Watson says nothing. It takes her a full minute to digest the scene before her. As a child, she witnessed a car crash, at traffic lights, near her home in Wisconsin. That incident changed her life, eventually leading to her first job: the local paper. Its impression has never left her. She had hoped never to see such physical evidence of pain on a human being again, but here it is, in front of her.

Saul, standing, remains silent, and allows her to fully absorb his condition. At last, he speaks, his voice hesitant and cracking with the strain. 'This is the work of Bovar. They found me ... beat me ... left me for dead. I've left hospital. You can see.' He spreads his hands open in front of her. They too are covered in deep cuts and bruising.

'Sit down, for God's sake.' The words catch in Natalie's mouth, as though her own breath is hard to come by. She tries to appraise the situation coolly, dispassionately, professionally, as should a seasoned newspaper journalist and editor of a renowned, national broadsheet. She fails. 'What's this got to do with Bovar?'

'They didn't know it was me.' Saul had run out of words. His throat is excruciatingly painful, despite ingesting large quantities of the pills. He feels sick, unstable. He points weakly at the water jug, eyes pleading, despite his pride.

Natalie pours him a glass. 'Saul, this is torment for you ' – her voice is full of compassion now – ' and I don't want to prolong this, but why have you come in?'

Clutching at the desk, Saul gasps, with staccato

vehemence, 'Diamonds, fraud, Bovar, Bychkov, Vasiliev. Please.' He pushes the USB across her desk, with a note in handwriting like the trail of a drug-crazed spider trying to weave a web. The message is clear: he is spent.

'I'll call an editorial meeting. You need to rest. Leave it to me. This will happen. Now. I'm so sorry.'

The slow trek back to the Range Rover is agonizing but, as Albie folds him onto the leather of the back seat, Saul feels nothing but gratitude.

Xenia is waiting in the car, iron-faced, containing a world of pain and confusion. As soon as they set off, her tears begin to fall, coursing in waves. 'I've known her for so long. I believed in her. The betrayal. Over all these years.'

Saul can only listen from the back seat. Albie, between gear changes, extends his arm to rest on Xenia's trembling frame.

Saul comes and goes, comes and goes, dimly comprehending Zee's distress in the front seat, then falls asleep as soon as he senses the welcome monotony of the motorway. He can't process the information about Polly in any way other than contingent on his storyline. *It's too much. One day, perhaps, not now.*

The last words he remembers hearing in the car, before waking a day later, between fresh sheets, back in hospital, is Albie quoting his father, 'We should be proud of Saul. He made every effort, and that's a great thing.'

Two days later, *The Inquirer* breaks the story on its front page with, 'Fake Diamonds Flood Global Markets'.

Ends

AFTERWORD

If you've enjoyed COVER-UP, please leave a review on Amazon (QR code below). It's highly valuable to me as an author, and it will encourage others to identify a book worth reading.

Many thanks, Orlando

FICTION : FIGHTBACK

Reader reviews include:

'A gripping, page-turning, contemporary political eco-thriller.'

'Brilliant observation of mainstream corruption.'

'Meticulously researched, intriguing and only too believable'

'...modern, interesting and fun...' **The Independent**

A pulsating novel set in modern-day Cornwall.

QR code for the print edition of FIGHTBACK

NON-FICTION : ESPRESSO

'crisp, refreshing and thought-provoking'

'A treasure trove of erudite, eccentric, nourishing and highly engaging short think-pieces'

'Loved every one of these finely crafted jewels'

Short, entertaining essays on the way we live today.

QR code for the print edition of ESPRESSO volume two

THANKS

Thank you (in alphabetical order), to Steve Andrews, Charles Beazley, Patricia Farrell, Jeremy Hurst, Piers Kimber, Dave Loewy, David Lye, Julyan Rawlings, Lord Shaw, John Stock, Nicholas Storey, Ray Todd, and Tom Varcoe.

Without their generous support and specialized knowledge, this book would not be as it is.

My deepest thanks go to Boo, for her unfailing wisdom, and shining example of fortitude.

Thank you, for choosing to read COVER-UP.

Printed in Great Britain
by Amazon